Penguin Classics of World Art

The Complete Paintings of Leonardo da Vinci

Leonardo was born in Vinci on 15 April 1452, the natural son of a Florentine notary. He was one of the greatest Renaissance men, and his genius was such that he virtually discovered the circulation of the blood, projected aircraft and anticipated the submarine, although none of these inventions were completed. Similarly, he left thousands of drawings but few paintings, only four of which – *The Adoration of the Magi, St Jerome, The Last Supper* and *The Mona Lisa* – are unequivocally believed to have been done by him.

Leonardo was apprenticed to Verrocchio and employed in his workshop in Florence between 1472 and 1476, during which time he painted, among other works, the *Annunciation*s now in the Uffizi and the Louvre. In 1482/3, leaving *The Adoration of the Magi* unfinished, he moved to Milan, having written the now famous letter to Lodovico Svorza, Il Moro, the Duke, in which he offered his services as a great military and civil engineer, also adding that 'I would undertake the commission of the bronze horse, which will endow with immortal glory and eternal honour the auspicious memory of your father and of the illustrious house of Svorza . . .' Leonardo remained in Milan until 1499, undertaking various scientific and artistic commissions, notably *The Virgin of the Rocks,* and *The Last Supper* in the Church of S. M. delle Grazie. 'Often – I have seen and observed him myself –' wrote Bandello in 1497, 'he used to climb on his scaffolding early in the morning, because *The Last Supper* is somewhat high off the ground; he would keep the brush in his hand from sunrise to sunset and, forgetting to eat or drink, would go on painting. Then for three or four days he would not touch his work, but for one or two hours a day he would stand and merely look at it, examine and judge his own figures.' During this time in Milan Leonardo took the young boy Jacomo (nicknamed *il Salai*, the Devil) into his household. Described by Leonardo as a 'thieving, lying, obstinate glutton', *il Salai* was his master's disciple until his death. Between 1500 and 1506 Leonardo lived mainly in Florence, working as a military engineer for Cesare Borgia, and on a number of versions of the Madonna and Child with St Anne. His masterpiece, the *Mona Lisa*, 'La Gioconda', was painted at this time. In 1506 Leonardo returned to Milan, and was made *Peintre et Ingénieur* to Louis XII of France in 1507. Over the next few years he concentrated mainly on mathematical and scientific projects, going to live in the Vatican in Rome, and working under the patronage of Giuliano de' Medici between 1513 and 1515. His final masterpiece, probably done before he moved to France in 1517, was *St John the Baptist,* now in the Louvre. Leonardo died in 1519 at Cloux, near Amboise in France, in a château given to him by François I.

'Leonardo was really admirable and heavenly,' wrote Vasari, fifty years later. 'Nature favoured him so highly that to whatever he applied his thoughts or his mind he achieved such divine perfection in his works that nobody ever equalled their liveliness, their beauty or their charm.'

The Complete Paintings of

Leonardo da Vinci

Introduction by L. D. Ettlinger

Notes and catalogue by Angela Ottino della Chiesa

Penguin Books

Penguin Books Ltd, Harmondsworth, Middlesex, England
Viking Penguin Inc., 40 West 23rd Street, New York, New York 10010, U.S.A.
Penguin Books Australia Ltd, Ringwood, Victoria, Australia
Penguin Books Canada Ltd, 2801 John Street, Markham, Ontario, Canada L3R 1B4
Penguin Books (N.Z.) Ltd, 182–190 Wairau Road, Auckland 10, New Zealand

First published by Rizzoli Editore 1967
This translation first published in Great Britain by Weidenfeld & Nicolson 1969
Published in Penguin Books 1985

Copyright © by Rizzoli Editore, 1967
Translation and introduction Copyright © George Weidenfeld & Nicolson, 1969
All rights reserved

Printed in Italy

Photographic sources

Colour plates : Blauel, Munich ; Dita Herein, Vaduz ;
Kolowca Stanislaw, Cracow ; Librairie Flammarion,
Paris ; Mandel, Milan ; Scala, Florence ; Witty,
Sunbury-on-Thames.
Black and white illustrations : Rizzoli Archives, Milan ;
Soprintendenza alle Gallerie, Naples.

Introduction

Among Leonardo's notes is the draft of a letter to Lodovico il Moro in which the Florentine artist offers his services to the duke. It is a strange and disquieting document, even if we assume that it may have been written at a moment when Milan was threatened by war. For without giving away anything Leonardo speaks in dark and veiled terms – but without a trace of self-doubt – about his ability to make 'endless means of attack and defence' – the stress clearly falling on the former, on mortars, catapults and 'other engines of wonderful efficacy'. Only right at the end of his letter, and almost casually, does he tell the duke that in time of peace he can give perfect satisfaction in architecture, in conducting water from one place to another, in sculpture and painting. A few years later when, after the French conquest of Milan, Leonardo had returned to Florence, we hear that the master was absorbed in some mathematical problems and would not receive anyone wishing to purchase a picture, while assistants were busy with paintings he had designed. Later still, during the second decade of the sixteenth century, when he was the Pope's honoured guest in the Belvedere of the Vatican Palace, we learn of experiments with mirrors (and of quarrels with the German workmen making them), of anatomical studies, of a book on the human voice, of geological enquiries and of plans for draining the Pontine Marshes. Nothing came of all this and, surrounded by the recent masterpieces of Bramante, Michelangelo and Raphael, Leonardo amused himself by decking out a lizard so that it might look like a miniature dragon. When during the closing years of his life he lived at Cloux at the invitation of François I visitors admired three of his paintings (though none of them recent since a paralysis in the right hand made it impossible for him to handle a brush) but they were astounded even more by 'an infinite number of volumes on anatomy, machinery, the nature of water and on other matters'. When finally only a few days before his death Leonardo drew up his will he left to his friend and pupil Francesco Melzi 'all the books the testator owns at present, and the tools ... connected with his profession as a painter'. These books can only have been the many volumes of notes, memoranda and drawings amassed throughout a life time. Again they are given precedence and painting takes second place.

All this speaks of an odd attitude from a man whom the contemporaries called one of the most excellent painters of the day, who stood for Vasari at the threshold of artistic fulfilment as the harbinger of the *terza maniera*, the High Renaissance, who after all left posterity two of the most famous paintings of all times, *The Mona Lisa* and *The Last Supper*. How can we resolve the apparent paradox?

It has become fashionable to speak of 'Leonardo the artist' *and* 'Leonardo the scientist' as if he had been some schizophrenic genius torn between two disparate pursuits and therefore rarely, if ever, able to accomplish anything in either. But Leonardo's own contemporaries, though impatient of his volatility, seem never to have made this distinction, and to the master himself such a dichotomy would have been incomprehensible. To say that as 'a man of the Renaissance' (whatever that phrase may mean) he believed that a painter needed the aid of anatomy, perspective, optics and so forth is not a proper answer. In fact, these alleged 'scientific' studies of Renaissance artists were a fashion confined to a small circle. In any case, Michelangelo and Raphael – to name only two outstanding examples – did not share these interests but were great artists nonetheless. Leonardo's inquiries were rooted in his personality, not in some tendency of the age, and many of his notes and drawings having nothing to do with the tasks awaiting painters of his time. They are not a vast store from which to draw raw materials for his art, nor was his art simply a finely distilled compound of observation and imagination.

In fact, many of Leonardo's drawings are different from those of his contemporaries and those by artists from any other period. Of course, there are among them rapid sketches from life, portraits, quick notes for compositions, elaborate cartoons, drapery studies, designs for machines and buildings, drawings of plants and animals, anatomical and proportion studies. But it is their nature which is so often peculiar. The plans of buildings grow before our eyes like the cells of some organism, plants appear on the same sheet both in bud and in flower (yet these drawings were hardly meant to be illustrations in some text-book on botany), trees are drawn schematically to demonstrate the principle of growth, there is a drawing of the peaceful Arno valley, and there are the cataclysmic visions of utter physical destruction of the world. The grotesque heads – to call them caricatures is a misnomer – are combinations and variations of human forms creating a morphological sequence of types. The anatomical drawings demonstrate not only the position of muscles and tendons or the bone structure, they also show the embryo in its mother's womb and a bare skull, – the beginning and end of life. All these drawings are concerned not just with the collection of visual data useful to the painter but with the processes of life, with growth and decay, whether in plants, beasts, man, or the world at large. *Mutatis mutandis* the same is true of Leonardo's designs for his various mechanical contrivances which are so often engines of construction or destruction.

Leonardo's notes should be considered in the same context. It is perhaps a pity that we have got used to thinking of them (or at least of very many of them) as if they had been written in preparation for some comprehensive treatise on painting. But it should be remembered that the huge manuscript known as *Trattato della Pittura* is not an autograph. It was compiled in the sixteenth century, probably by Francesco Melzi, from no less than eighteen of the original note-books. The result certainly is a labour of love, but nevertheless this gathering divided into eight chapters is too rigid, too much like a textbook to reveal Leonardo's truly dynamic nature. Maybe the compiler himself felt doubts about the scope of such a treatise, for there are empty leaves at the end of each chapter, surely for the later addition of relevant material. Furthermore the chapters on elementary anatomy, proportion, on light and shade deal with topics every painter must know, but a whole section on clouds introduces a subject certainly dear to Leonardo, while hardly relevant to the practice of art in the sixteenth century. All this is not surprising, since among Leonardo's many schemes for research no complete programme for a treatise on painting has been found. Poussin realized the weakness of the *Trattato* as a systematic essay on painting and advised against even partial publication. While it is of course

true that Leonardo made copious notes about many aspects of painting – both technical and theoretical – even their scope goes far beyond a handbook for students or artists.

Leonardo repeatedly expressed his scorn for those who relied on book learning and the authority of older writers. By contrast he claims that his work is the result of 'simple and plain experience which is the true mistress'. With a characteristic mixture of pride and contempt he bursts out: 'Though I have no power to quote from authors as they have, I shall rely on a far bigger and more worthy thing: on experience, the instructress of their masters. They strut about puffed up and pompous, decked out and adorned not with their own labours, but by those of others, and they will not even allow me my own. And if they despise me who am an inventor, how much more should they be blamed who are not inventors but trumpeters and reciters of the works of others'. The most interesting claim in this passage is Leonardo's assertion that he is an *inventor*, clearly meaning not so much the man who devises some new gadget but a discoverer in a far more general sense. His concept of the painter and his task must have been one of these 'discoveries'.

Through his notes and drawings Leonardo has left us an uneasy heritage. The same is true of his few paintings, which lack the poise and calm of a Raphael or the almost physical force of a Michelangelo. The *sfumato* – the suggestive smoke-like contour – is as much a technical feature of his art as it is a characteristic of his personality. All his life he observed and recorded through word and picture natural phenomena and mechanical contrivances of every kind. Often enough they seem remote from any conceivable artistic task. Yet in the end his mind seems always to return to an apparently simple yet obsessive question: what is painting? He had straightforward and technical definitions such as: 'Painting is a composition of light and shade, combined with all the various kinds of simple and compound colours', or 'The first task of a painter is to make a flat surface appear like a relief and its parts as if detached from the ground ...'. But when considering the role of the painter in a less technical sense he had a definition making him an 'inventor' of a rather special kind: 'The painter is lord of all types of people and of all things. If he wishes to see beauties that charm him it lies in his power to create them, and if he wishes to see monstrosities that are frightful, buffoonish or ridiculous, or pitiable he can be lord and god thereof ... If he wants valleys, if he wants from high mountain tops to unfold a great plain extending down to the sea's horizon, he is lord to do so ... In fact whatever exists in the universe, in essence, in appearance, in the imagination, the painter has first in his mind and then in his hand'.

An urge more fundamental than the desire to give a faithful rendering of the visible world must have driven a man who set himself such an aim. We should make some allowance for overstatement since Leonardo seems to have expressed himself in this way when the relative merits of painting, sculpture, music and poetry were debated at the Sforza court, and some of these discussions may well have been sophisticated banter. Still, set within the framework of Leonardo's thought, we cannot miss the serious undertones of this definition of the painter as a god-like inventor. It is also worth noting in this context that the many descriptions of *The Mona Lisa* from Vasari to our own day – and they contain not a few prose poems of rare distinction – are concerned as much with the creative power of Leonardo's brush as with the perplexing personality he has created.

Leonardo's thinking about the power of the artist can also furnish the clue to the famous enigmatic self-portrait in red chalk. It has often been remarked that on it the master looks older than his age – he can have been only about sixty when he made this drawing – and in consequence some critics have doubted whether

it is a likeness of himself. Other good reasons apart, however, this portrait perfectly fits the role in which Leonardo had cast himself. A venerable old man with a long white beard, the severe eyes shaded under bushy brows, was the traditional type for representing philosophers, prophets and also God. Nobody would suggest seriously, of course, that Leonardo has drawn himself consciously in the semblance of the Almighty, but we must remember his claim that the painter contends with nature and that painting is related to God. This imposing sage who seems to have come from some other world has something of the indefinable mien of a magus, of a one who through discovering the laws of the universe knows how to manipulate them.

Knowledge of nature and its processes clearly meant power to Leonardo, that is the artist's power to create with pen and brush a second nature. He was not a scientist, in spite of his far flung research, for he never wanted to know for the sake of knowledge. Nor was he an artist in the modern sense since he was not interested in art for art's sake. When he wrote: ... 'the painter is lord of all types of people and of all things', he spoke of those powers which as an artist he claimed for himself. And yet he never finished his investigations and rarely his paintings for in the end he must have shrunk from the very power which his creations might give him. The most revealing of his notes reads: 'One should not desire the impossible'.

L. D. ETTLINGER

7

An outline of the artist's critical history

Like Raphael's, and even more than Michelangelo's, Leonardo's critical and literary reputation has been consistently high for four centuries. This is all the more surprising if we think that his achievement as a scientist was only discovered during the first decades of the last century and therefore his unchanging fame has rested for nearly three centuries merely on his few painted works, some incomplete, some destroyed, some only rough sketches. And our surprise grows when we see the uninterrupted stream of praise, the force of legend and the wishful thinking of famous collectors result in attributing to his genius works by his Florentine contemporaries or followers, such as Lorenzo di Credi, or by Lombard disciples such as Ambrogio de Predis, Boltraffio, Luini, all very far removed from the utter perfection and inventive originality of Leonardo. Sometimes, the praise is directed at works by other hands, sometimes at genuine works of his which the writer has never seen, but only knows from hearsay. We must conclude that the fascination exerted by the painter of the most famous picture in the world, *The Mona Lisa*, and of the most studied wall-painting, *The Last Supper*, was kept alive through the ages not so much by the knowledge of his works, but above all by a literary tradition to which every famous writer contributed. There is not a single travel book about Italy or Europe, however vague or incompetent, not a single writing about art criticism or technique, which does not mention him, not a single critic who ignores him, not a single scholar or artist who does not discuss him. Consequently, it is impossible to give a critical anthology faithfully mirroring this miscellaneous accumulation of references, monographs, books which, piled up together, would form a large library. Scholars who have devoted their work above all and exclusively to Leonardo, such as Amoretti, Bossi, Calvi, Verga, Beltrami, Richter, Solmi, Poggi, Uzielli, Duhem, Seidlitz, would be found side by side with critics whose pages have illuminated our research, from Müller-Walde to A. Venturi, Jacobsen, Thiis, Bode, Clark, Suida, Berenson, Goldscheider, Castelfranco, Heydenreich, and with poets and writers from Goethe to Stendhal, Pater, Barrès, Valéry, Cassirer, Garin, Brion. All of them gather round the famous name, each bringing the tribute of his own judgment and sensitivity. The following extracts, therefore, are not even a tiny mirror trying to reflect faithfully a huge landscape; they are, rather, flowers picked here and there in that extensive literature.

Often – I have seen and observed him myself – he [Leonardo] used to climb on his scaffolding early in the morning, because *The Last Supper* is somewhat high off the ground; he would keep the brush in his hand from sunrise to sunset and, forgetting to eat or drink, would go on painting. Then for three or four days he would not touch his work, but for one or two hours a day, he would stand and merely look at it, examine it and judge his own figures. I have also seen him (according to the way in which his whim or fancy took him) set out at midday, when the sun is in Leo, from Corte Vecchia where he was working on his remarkable clay horse and come straight to the convent delle Gratie: there, he would climb on the scaffolding, take up his brush, add one or two strokes to one of the figures, and go off again. M. BANDELLO, *Novelle*, 1497

The famous works of art which the Master Leonardo da Vinci, your compatriot, has left in Italy and above all in this city [Milan] have particularly endeared him to all those who have seen them, even though they never saw him. And we must confess that we were among those who loved him before meeting him face to face. But since we met him and found out for ourselves his virtues, we notice that his name, which is celebrated for his paintings, is far from receiving all the fame it deserves for his very high virtues ... C. D'AMBOISE, letter from Milan to the governors of Florence, 1506

... Another of the greatest painters in the world [Leonardo] looks down on this art in which he is unequalled and has taken up the learning of philosophy, in which he has such strange thoughts and new fancies that even with all his writing, he cannot describe them. B. CASTIGLIONE, *Il Cortegiano*, 1528

His genius was so rare and universal that it can be said that nature worked a miracle on his behalf: she gave him not only physical beauty – which was remarkable – but many rare gifts. He was learned in mathematics and equally in perspective, he worked as a sculptor and his drawings surpassed all others by far. He made many beautiful inventions, but left very few paintings, because it is said that he could never be satisfied with his own work. He was most eloquent in his speech, and played the lyre uncommonly well and taught that instrument to Atalante Migliorotti. He applied himself with delight to the study of the properties of plants and he was knowledgeable about wells, waterworks and other inventions, and his mind was never at rest but always devising new things. 'ANONIMO GADDIANO', Elaboration of the *Libro di Antonio Billi*, 1537–42

... In fact, theory springs from the brain, but practise depends on the hands, and that is why Leonardo Vinci who was most learned was never satisfied with what he did, achieved perfection with only a few works and often said that the reason was that his hand could not follow his intellect. S. SERLIO, *Il secondo libro di perspectiva*, 1551

Leonardo was Michelangelo's equal in all things, but his spirit aimed so high that he was never satisfied with what he had created. L. DOLCE, *Dialogo della pittura*, 1557

Leonardo was really admirable and heavenly ... Nature favoured him so highly that to whatever he applied his thoughts or his mind, he achieved such divine perfection in his works that nobody ever equalled their liveliness, their beauty or their charm.

We find that Leonardo, through his understanding of art, began many works, none of which he completed, since he felt that his hand could not reach the artistic perfection conceived by his mind ... One of the striking aspects of his talent was that to give the maximum relief to his works he used dark shadows and, to produce the darkest possible backgrounds, he looked for blacks which would give deeper shadows and be darker than other blacks, making the clear colours look more vivid by contrast. Thus, he succeeded in obtaining shades which, since they did not remain clear, gave the impression that his subjects were seen by night rather than daylight. But it was all done to obtain more relief and to achieve artistic perfection ... In the art of painting, he brought to the technique of colouring in oils a certain darkness, from which modern painters have learnt to give a great power and relief to their figures. G. VASARI, *Le Vite*, 1568

Vinci was inspired by nobility of spirit, a gifted and clear imagination, the nature of knowledge, thought and action, and wisdom and also by beautiful faces, by justice, reason, judgment, the dividing of right from wrong, the height of the light, the depths of darkness and ignorance, the great glory of truth and of charity, the queen of all virtues.

And thus although Leonardo shook with emotion whenever he began painting, he never finished anything he started because he thought of the greatness of art and always found mistakes in works which to others seemed miraculous.

Leonardo seems to have been always afraid of making things too bright, as though he had kept light in reserve for a better occasion, and he tried to intensify darkness, to keep the balance between the two. With that technique, he represented faces and bodies so admirably that nature could do no better. In this he had no equal and we can say in one word that his light was divine. G. P. LOMAZZO, *Idea del Tempio della pittura*, 1590

L. Davinci [*sic*] had a very finished painting technique with a way of spreading the colours evenly ... which was peculiar to him. From what I could see, his light and shadow seem to be melted or confused with each other and most of the protruding parts of the bodies are rounded, particularly small parts, as can be seen in several of his paintings, above all in two of them: *The Mona Lisa* and a *Flora* which used to be in the collection of the late Queen Mother, Marie de' Medici. However, some of the works by him which I have seen still derive from the manner of Perugino, Giovanni Bellini and many of those ancient painters, but, in my opinion, are of a much higher quality. A. BOSSE, *Sentimens sur la distinction des diverses manières de peinture ...*, 1649

Because of his high ideas of perfection and beauty, Leonardo tried to finish his works beyond the extreme limits of artistic possibilities and drew figures which are not really natural. He marked the outline very strongly, made endless corrections of small details, and used too much black for the shadows. But through his own peculiar gifts for draughtsmanship and for the harmony of lighting effects, he gave all objects a relief which deceives the eye. A. FÉLIBIEN, *Entretiens sur les Vies et les Ouvrages des plus excellents Peintres Anciens et Modernes*, 1666

I found that work [*The Last Supper*] beautiful, but of a male, stern and austere beauty which is not easily appreciated in France. J. P. GROSLEY, *Nouveaux Mémoires sur l'Italie et les italiens par deux gentilshommes suédois*, 1764

Leonardo da Vinci was born before Buonarotti and his genius was less forceful, less wide but gentler ... He had two manners, one full of dark tones which makes the light tones stand out; ... and another quieter manner in half-tones ... In every style of his, his graceful draughtsmanship, soulful expression and subtlety of brushwork are remarkable. L. LANZI, *Storia pittorica dell'Italia*, 1792

... although he was a universal genius, Leonardo was great above all as a painter. Perfectly proportioned, compared with ordinary specimens of humanity, he seemed to embody its ideal. Clarity and acuity of vision depend more particularly on the intellect, and a clear intelligence characterised him. He never gave way to the extreme impulses of his own original and incomparable talent, but kept every spontaneous and casual transport under control because he wanted every line to be the result of thorough reflection. From his studies on pure proportions to the extraordinary and contradictory shapes of the most hybrid monsters, everything had to look natural and rational.
W. GOETHE, *Italienische Reise*, 1786–8

Such was the dawn of modern art, when Leonardo da Vinci broke forth with a splendour which distanced former excellence: made up of all the elements that constitute the essence of genius, favoured by education, and circumstances, all ear, all eye, all grasp; painter, poet, sculptor, anatomist, architect, engineer, chemist, machinist, musician, man of science, and sometimes empiric, he laid hold of every beauty in the enchanted circle, but without exclusive attachment to one, dismissed in her turn each. Fitter to scatter hints than to teach by example, he wasted life, insatiate, in experiment. To a capacity which at once penetrated the principle and real aim of the art, he joined an inequality of fancy that at one moment lent him wings for the pursuit of beauty, and the next, flung him on the ground to crawl after deformity: we owe him chiaroscuro with all its magic, we owe him caricature with all its incongruities. His notions of the most elaborate finish and his want of perseverance were at least equal... H. FUSELI, *Lectures* (II), 1801

He used soft, melancholy tones, full of shadows, devoid of sharpness in the bright colours, and most effective in the *chiaroscuro*, which if they had not existed, should have been invented for such a subject [*The Last Supper*]. H. BEYLE [STENDHAL], *Histoire de la peinture en Italie*, 1817

... he is more realistic than those of his predecessors who recognize the demands of reality, but at the same time, his is free and sublime as few artists have been, through the centuries. J. BURCKHARDT, *Der Cicerone*, 1855

Leonardo da Vinci, like a deep, dark mirror, within which charming angels with a sweet, mysterious smile, appear in the shade of the glaciers and pine trees which enclose their landscape. CH. BAUDELAIRE, *Les Fleurs du Mal*, 1857

Almost a contemporary of Ghirlandaio, and a fellow-disciple of Lorenzo di Credi and Perugino ... he discarded traditional fifteenth-century painting and without mistakes, without weaknesses, without exaggeration and almost in one leap, he reached a wise and clever naturalism, equally remote from servile imitation and from an empty and fanciful idealism. How strange! The most methodical of men, who among the masters of that time was most concerned with methods of execution and taught them so accurately that the works of his best pupils are invariably confused with his own, this man, whose 'manner' is so characteristic, is never 'rhetorical'. Always watching nature and referring to it, he never repeats himself; the most learned of artists is also the most natural, and neither of his two rivals, Michelangelo and Raphael, deserves this praise as much as he does. E. DELACROIX, *Journal*, 1857–63

He towered above all other artists through the strength and the nobility of his talent which was a synthesis of idealism and realism ... No other artist penetrated so deeply into the mysteries of science ... However execution did not do justice to the greatness of the conception and, because of the apparent disorder in which he left the fruit of his own meditations and inspirations, neither his contemporaries nor posterity gave him his due. A. E. RIO, *L'art chrétien*, 1861

There may not be in the world another example of a genius so universal, so inventive, so incapable of fulfilment, so full of yearning for the infinite, so naturally refined, so far ahead of his own century and the following centuries. His figures reveal an incredible sensitivity and intellect; they are full of unexpressed ideas and feelings. Next to them, Michelangelo's characters are mere heroic athletes, Raphael's virgins only placid girls whose unawakened souls have never known life. Leonardo's virgins feel and think through every feature and every expression; it takes some time to establish a dialogue with them; not that their feeling is not clear enough, on the contrary it bursts out of the whole figure, but it is too subtle, too complicated, too much outside and beyond ordinary experience, too unfathomable, too unexplainable. Their immobility and their silence allow us to guess two or three layers of thought and other deeper thoughts,

hiding behind the most remote layer; we vaguely discern this intimate, secret world, like a delicate, unknown vegetation below the depths of a transparent water. H. TAINE, *Voyage en Italie*, 1866

Again; in the Leonardo sketches, many parts are lost in obscurity, or are left intentionally uncertain and mysterious, even in the light, and you might at first imagine some permission of escape had been here given you from the terrible law of delineation. But the slightest attempts to copy them will show you that the terminal lines are inimitably subtle, unaccusably true, and filled by gradations of shade so determined and measured that the addition of a grain of lead or chalk as large as the filament of a moth's wing would make an appreciable difference in them.

This is grievous, you think, and hopeless? No, it is delightful and full of hope: delightful, to see what marvellous things can be done by men; and full of hope, if your hope is the right one, of being one day able to rejoice more in what others have done, than in what you can yourself do, and more in the strength that is for ever above you, than in that you can ever attain. JOHN RUSKIN, *Lectures on Art*, 1870

Other artists have been as careless of present or future applause, in self-forgetfulness, or because they set moral or political ends above the end of art; but in him this solitary culture of beauty seems to have hung upon a kind of self-love, and a carelessness in the work of art of all but art itself. Out of the secret place of a unique temperament he brought strange blossoms and fruits hitherto unknown; and for him, the novel impression conveyed, the exquisite effect woven, counted as an end in itself – a perfect end ...

La Gioconda is, in the truest sense, Leonardo's masterpiece, the revealing instance of his mode of thought and work. In suggestiveness, only the *Melancholia* of Dürer is comparable to it; and no crude symbolism disturbs the effect of its subdued and graceful mystery ... She is older than the rocks among which she sits; like the vampire, she has been dead many times, and learned the secrets of the grave; and has been a diver in deep seas, and keeps their fallen day about her; and trafficked for strange webs with Eastern merchants and, as Leda, was the mother of Helen of Troy, and, as Saint Anne, the mother of Mary; and all this has been to her but as the sound of lyres and flutes, and lives only on the delicacy with which it has moulded the changing lineaments, and tinged the eyelids and the hands. The fancy of a perpetual life, sweeping together ten thousand experiences, is an old one; and modern philosophy has conceived the idea of humanity as wrought upon by, and summing up in itself, all modes of thought and life. Certainly Lady Lisa might stand as the embodiment of the old fancy, the symbol of the modern idea. W. PATER, *The Renaissance*, 1873

Often and often he made vast preparations and accomplished nothing. It is well known how the Prior of S. Maria delle Grazie complained that Lionardo stood for days looking at his fresco, and for weeks never came near it; how the monks of the Annunziata at Florence were cheated out of their painting, for which elaborate designs had yet been made; how Leo x, seeing him mix oils with varnish to make a new medium, exclaimed, 'Alas! this man will do nothing; he thinks of the end before he makes a beginning.' A good answer to account for the delay was always ready on the painter's lips, as that the man of genius works most when his hands are idlest; Judas, sought in vain through all the thieves' resorts in Milan, is not found; I cannot hope to see the face of Christ except in Paradise. Again, when an equestrian statue of Francesco Sforza had been modelled in all its parts, another model was begun because Da Vinci would fain show the warrior triumphing over a fallen foe. The first motive seemed to him tame; the second was unrealizable in bronze. 'I can do anything possible to man', he wrote to Lodovico Sforza, 'and as well as any living artist either in sculpture or painting.' But he would do nothing as taskwork, and his creative brain loved better to invent than to execute. 'Of a truth,' continues his biographer, 'there is good reason to believe that the very greatness of his most exalted mind, aiming at more than could be effected, was itself an impediment; perpetually seeking to add excellence to excellence and perfection to perfection. This was without doubt the true hindrance, so that, as our Petrarch has it, the work was retarded by desire.' At the close of that cynical and positive century, the spirit whereof was so well expressed by Cosimo de' Medici, Lionardo set before himself aims infinite instead of finite. His designs of wings to fly with symbolize his whole endeavour. He believed in solving the insoluble; and nature had so richly dowered him in the very dawntime of discovery, that he was almost justified in this delusion. Having caught the Proteus of the world, he tried to grasp him; but the god changed shape beneath his touch. Having surprised Silenus asleep, he begged from him a song; but the song Silenus sang was so marvellous in its variety, so subtle in its modulations, that Lionardo could do no more than recall scattered phrases. His Proteus was the spirit of the Renaissance. The Silenus from whom he forced the song was the double nature of man and of the world. A. SYMONDS, *The Renaissance in Italy*, 1877

Thirsty for truth, he borrows from nature all the elements of his works, which he eagerly combines according to the suggestions of his imagination. The acuteness of his mind is not dissociated from his exquisite perceptions, from his refined and subtle emotions. His intuitions are directly transmitted to his mind, and his ideas to his heart. The dreams of other men are vague forms, fluctuating fantasies, but his dreaming is a surging of clear thoughts which he masters immediately. His genius has nothing in common with madness; it is health itself, the expression of a powerful spirit, the balanced and happy combination of all human faculties. The secret of his works lies in a decanted mixture of observation and imagination, of analysis and emotion, of nature and spirit: the psychological reality of a man who knows that the human spirit is present everywhere and must manifest itself everywhere. G. SÉAILLES, *Léonard de Vinci, l'artiste et le savant*, 1892

Outside Velazquez, and perhaps, when at their best, Rembrandt and Degas, we shall seek in vain for tactile values so stimulating and so convincing as those of his *Mona Lisa;* outside Degas, we shall not find such supreme mastery over the art of movement as in the unfinished *Epiphany* in the Uffizi; and if Leonardo has been left far behind as a painter of light, no one has succeeded in conveying by means of light and shade a more penetrating feeling of mystery and awe than he in his *Virgin of the Rocks*. Add to all this a feeling for beauty and significance that have scarcely ever been approached ... Leonardo is the one artist of whom it may be said with perfect literalness: Nothing that he touched but turned into a thing of eternal beauty. Whether it be the cross-section of a skull, the structure of a weed, or a study of muscles, he, with his feeling for line and for light and shade, for ever transmuted it into life-communicating values ...

... Great though he was as a painter, he was no less renowned as a sculptor and architect, musician and improviser ... Painting was to him so little of a pre-occupation that we must regard it as merely a mode of expression used at moments by a man of universal genius, who recurred to it only when he had no more absorbing occupation, and only when it could express what nothing else could, the highest spiritual through the highest material significance. B. BERENSON, *The Italian Painters of the Renaissance*, 1896

Of all Renaissance artists, Leonardo was the one who most enjoyed the world. All phenomena captivated him – physical life and human emotions, the forms of plants and animals, the sight of the crystal-clear stream with the pebbles in its bed. To him, the one-sideness of the mere figure-painter was incomprehensible.

He is a born aristocrat among painters, sensitive to delicacy, with a feeling for fine hands, for the charm of transparent stuffs, for smooth skin, and above all, he loves beautiful, soft, rippling hair. In Verrocchio's *Baptism* he painted a few tufts of grasses, and one sees at once that they were painted by him, for no one else had quite this feeling for the natural grace of growing things ... He discovered the painterly charm of the surfaces of things and yet he can think as a physicist and an anatomist. Qualities which seem mutually exclusive are combined in him: the tireless observation and collection of data of the student, and the most subtle artistic perception. As a painter, he is never content to accept things merely by their outward appearance: he throws himself into investigating, with the same passionate interest, inner structure and the factors governing the life of every created thing. He was the first artist to make a systematic study of proportion in men and animals and to investigate the mechanics of movements like walking, lifting, climbing, pulling, and it was he, too, who made the most comprehensive physiognomical studies and thought out a coherent system for the expression of emotions. For him, the painter is like a clear eye which surveys the world and takes all visible things for its domain. H. WÖLFFLIN, *Classic Art*, 1898

What Leonardo suggests in his drawings, he carries out in his paintings: air, light, movement. It is an achievement which, for centuries, had been realized through colour, and yet Leonardo uses no colour. He found in Florence a vivid colouring technique designed to add a precious texture to a solid surface. He discarded it because he was not interested in solid surfaces. His eye liked to rove through the wide horizons of open valleys, interrupted by hills, limited by mountains. What meaning had a solid surface in a far away vision of wide horizons? It was convenient for the representation of a human body seen from nearby. But Leonardo's eye wanted to see even the human figure from afar. From nearby, everything seems set; but the continuous shimmering of the atmosphere makes distant things seem lighter, as if they were suspended in mid-air. On peaceful evenings, when twilight muffles souls and objects, the horizon throbs gently. Twilight, atmosphere, the physical movement of every molecule in the universe, the spiritual vibration of a daydream, the vagueness of confused distant objects; he brought all these things to the human figure ... Form without form. Colour without colour. A chromatic vision of form, a formal rendering of colour. L. VENTURI, *La critica e l'arte di Leonardo da Vinci*, 1919

But it is with Leonardo da Vinci that the higher aspects of the scientific spirit first came into conflict with art. Doubtless this conflict is not fundamental nor final, but only an apparent result of human limitations; but to one who, like Leonardo, first had a Pisgah prospect of that immense territory, to the exploration of which four centuries of the intensest human effort have been devoted without yet getting in sight of its boundaries – to such a man it was almost inevitable that the scientific content of art should assume an undue significance. Up till Leonardo one can say that the process of digesting the new-found material into aesthetic form had kept pace with observation, though already in Verrocchio there is a sign of yielding to the crude phenomenon. But with Leonardo himself the organising faculty begins to break down under the stress of new matter. Leonardo himself shared to the full the Florentine passion for abstraction, but it was inevitable that he should be dazzled and fascinated by the vast prospects that opened before his intellectual gaze. It was inevitable that where such vast masses of new particulars revealed themselves to his curiosity their claim for investigation should be the most insistent. Not but what Leonardo did recognize the necessity for his art of some restriction and choice. His keen observation had revealed to him the whole gamut of atmospheric colour which first became a material for design under Monet and his followers. But having described a picture which would exactly correspond to a French painting of 1870, he rejects the whole of this new material as unsuitable for art. But even his rejection was not really a recognition of the claims of form, but only, alas! of another scientific trend with which his mind had become possessed. It was his almost prophetic vision of the possibilities of psychology which determined more than anything else the lines of his work. In the end almost everything was subordinated to the idea of a kind of psychological illustration of dramatic themes – an illustration which was not to be arrived at by an instinctive reconstruction from within, but by deliberate analytic observation. Now in so far as the movements of the soul could be interpreted by movements of the body as a whole, the new material might lend itself readily to plastic construction, but the minuter and even more psychologically significant movements of facial expression demanded a treatment which hardly worked for aesthetic unity. It involved a new use of light and shade, which in itself tended to break down the fundamental divisions of design, though later on Caravaggio and Rembrandt managed, not very successfully, to pull it round so as to become the material for the basic rhythm. And in any case the analytic trend of Leonardo's mind became too much accentuated to allow of a successful synthesis. Michelangelo, to some extent, and Raphael still more, did, of course, do much to re-establish a system of design on an enlarged basis which would admit of some of Leonardo's new content, but one might hazard the speculation that European art has hardly yet re-

covered from the shock which Leonardo's passion for psychological illustration delivered. Certainly literalism and illustration have through all these centuries been pressing dangers to art – dangers which it has been the harder to resist in that they allow of an appeal to that vast public to whom the language of form is meaningless. ROGER FRY, *The Art of Florence*, 1919

Undoubtedly, particularly at the beginning of his career, the sculptor within him fought with the painter. He was a Florentine to the marrow, even though he was shrewder, more adaptable, more intelligent than his predecessors. Later he became interested in painterly problems as he was working on scientific ones; which accounts for new tendencies in his work, for features unknown of his contemporaries. The transition from precise details and clear outlines to gradations of light and shade and to a dense *sfumato* fits in with a general tendency of Renaissance painting; but whilst this development took other painters two or three generations, it matured, in Leonardo's case, within twenty or thirty years.

No artist was quicker to assimilate expressive forms inherited from the past and to create new ones; nobody knew better how to make form into the living vehicle of his artistic idea. Another Florentine characteristic was his obstination in finding in every object its most striking points and characteristic features: the fundamental note in Leonardo's art is essentially Florentine; but he was to find harmonies of a richness unknown until then in the art of his home-town. O. SIRÉN, *Léonard de Vinci*, 1928

In the Renaissance which brought together all human activities, art meant science, art meant truth to life: Leonardo was a great figure because he embodied the epic endeavour of Italian art to conquer universal values: he who combined within himself the fluctuating sensitivity of the artist and the deep wisdom of the scientist, he, the poet and the master. A. VENTURI, *L'arte di Leonardo*, in the 'Enciclopedia Italiana', XX, 1934

In his *Mona Lisa*, the individual, a sort of miraculous creation of nature, represents at the same time the species: the portrait goes beyond its social limitations and acquires a universal meaning. Although Leonardo worked on this picture as a scholar and thinker, not only as a painter and poet, the scientific and philosophical aspects of his research inspired no following. But the formal aspect – the new presentation, the nobler attitude and the increased dignity of the model – had a decisive influence over Florentine portraits of the next twenty years, over the classical portrait ... With his *Mona Lisa*, Leonardo created a new formula, at the same time more monumental and more lively, more concrete and yet more poetic than that of his predecessors ... Before him, portraits had lacked mystery; artists only represented outward appearances without any soul, or, if they showed the soul, they tried to express it through gestures, symbolic objects or inscriptions. *The Mona Lisa* alone is a living enigma: the soul is there, but inaccessible.

This poetic mystery is increased by the close unity of the figure with the background landscape ... CH. DE TOLNAY, *Remarques sur la Joconde*, in the 'Revue des Arts', 1951

The English critic, above all, is embarrassed by Pater's immortal passage ringing in his ears, and reminding him that anything he may write will be poor and shallow by comparision. Yet the *Mona Lisa* is one of those works of art which each generation must re-interpret. To follow M. Valery and to dismiss her smile as *un pli de visage*, is to admit defeat. It is also to misunderstand Leonardo, for the Mona Lisa's smile is the supreme example of that complex inner life, caught and fixed in durable material, which Leonardo in all his notes on the subject claims as one of the chief aims of his art. A quarry so shy must be approached with every artifice. We can well believe Vasari's story, that Leonardo 'retained musicians who played and sang and continually jested in order to take away that melancholy that painters are used to give to their portraits'; and we must remember the passage in the *Trattato* (p 135) which describes how the face yields its subtlest expression when seen by evening light in stormy weather. In this shunning of strong sunlight we feel once more the anti-classical, we might say the un-Mediterranean nature of Leonardo. 'Set her for a moment', says Pater, 'beside one of those white Greek goddesses, or beautiful women of antiquity, and how would they be troubled by this beauty into which the soul with all its maladies has passed.' In its essence Mona Lisa's smile is a gothic smile, the smile of the queens and saints at Rheims or Bamberg, but since Leonardo's ideal of beauty was touched by pagan antiquity, she is smoother and more fleshly than gothic saints. They are transparent, she is opaque. Their smiles are the pure illumination of the spirit; in hers there is something wordly, watchful and self-satisfied. K. CLARK, *Leonardo da Vinci*, 1952

Leonardo's sketches of the Deluge are symbolic of ... elementary forces seen at work in their final destructive stage: they are dismembering what they themselves had generated, shaped and set in motion, but they obey, in their very destruction, a higher necessity which commands that even the end of the world should take place according to certain harmonious rules.

The conclusions reached by Leonardo as a scientist were expressed through his artistic creations. Thus we see once more the grandiose unity and the close inter-relations of his scientific and his artistic thought ... He was clearly aware of all this himself, as we can see from his own words: 'Nature is full of infinite causes which were never part of human experience'. Until the very last moment of his life, Leonardo was imbued with the idea of a supernatural harmony which manifested itself in all forms and forces, everywhere and at all times, and even in the apparent chaos of the end of the world. He tried to find that harmony in all the phenomena observed by his inquisitive mind, and he tried to express it in all his works, through his art, which was the instrument of his research and of his science. L. H. HEYDENREICH, *Leonardo da Vinci*, in the 'Enciclopedia universale dell'arte', VIII, 1958

The brothers of San Francesco Grande were confronted with an altarpiece [*The Virgin of the Rocks*] which, needless to say, bore no resemblance to what they wanted and had commissioned and which moreover could only provoke amazement, disquiet and puzzlement from the congregation who would behold, on their favourite altar, such an enigmatic scene. The prophets who should have played a similar part to that of the saints and the Fathers of the Church in the *Pala Sforzesca* [by an anonymous Lombard painter, in the Brera] had been discarded; so had the

musician angels who should have surrounded the Virgin; those whom the master left for Ambrogio de Predis to execute, were relegated to the sides of the picture. For Leonardo knew that the secret music which pervades this composition cannot be heard if the eye of the listener is fixed on some static instrument. Therefore he deliberately avoided those beautiful groups of musician angels which had been commissioned and which Piero della Francesca or Bramantino enjoyed representing. If these angels had been present, the onlooker would imagine their music, but he would not *hear* it, he would merely think about it. For the music of the picture itself to rise and blossom fully in its elementary and supernatural harmony, the instruments must remain invisible, since the music of *The Virgin of the Rocks* comes from the water, the plants, the wind moving between the cracks in the rocks, the gestures of the characters, their smile, and no flute, no lyre, no lute could create such harmonies. The melody which we hear, and which the angels of De Predis try in vain and so indolently to follow, is the song of the earth, the rumbling of the elements, the message of that *Erdgeist* who once appeared to old Faustus and terrified him but who was so familiar to the young Leonardo that, from his childhood he lived on friendly terms with him, knowing that the soul of the artist and the soul of the world are one. M. BRION, *Léonard de Vinci*, 1959

Everything which gives value to human life leads to the awareness of its precariousness, and above all of its fundamental ambiguity ... This awareness of man's ambiguous position between the awful and the exquisite, between certainty and illusion, grew stronger with the years, in Leonardo. In his painted work, there is a parallel development of the use of *chiaroscuro*. Its principle was originally the interest in the contrast which emphasised opposite terms: *Le bellezze con le brutezze paiono più potenti l'una per l'altra.* (Beauty and ugliness seem all the more powerful because of each other). Therefore he enjoyed melting gradually 'soft lights into delightful shadows' and resolving in that way the conflict between line and modelling ... Of course, the *sfumato* is first of all the solution of a technical problem: it makes the forms stand out without brutal outlines or accented reliefs; it gives them a smooth, continuous quality ...

In painting, Leonardo dealt with the conflict of style with as much originality and decision as he did in intellectual problems. His solution is opposed to that of Botticelli who remained within the limits of Tuscan abstraction or to that of Ghirlandaio or even Piero di Cosimo who accumulated elements without assimilating them completely. When he claimed that painters must, like Giotto and Masaccio, be purely 'sons of nature', he meant that all problems of painting, at all stages, should be completely re-thought. The *sfumato* solved the difficulties of draughtsmanship by giving, through the enveloping atmosphere, unity to the forms in space; to ignore it would be 'to resemble those fine talkers who have nothing to say'. A. CHASTEL, *Art et Humanisme à Florence au temps de Laurent le Magnifique*, 1959

... Leonardo, if anyone, knew that the artist's desire to create, to bring forth a second reality, finds its inexorable limits in the restrictions of the medium. I feel we can watch an echo of the disillusionment with having created only a picture ... when we read in Leonardo's notes: 'Painters often fall into despair ... when they see that their paintings lack the roundness and the liveliness which we find in objects seen in the mirror ... but it is impossible for a painting to look as a mirror image ... except if you look at both with one eye only'.

Perhaps the passage betrays the ultimate reason for Leonardo's deep dissatisfaction with his art, his reluctance to reach the fatal moment of completion: all the artist's knowledge and imagination are of no avail, it is only a picture that he has been painting, and it will look flat. Small wonder that contemporaries describe him in his later years as most impatient of the brush and engrossed in mathematics. Mathematics was to help him to be the true maker. Today we read of Leonardo's project to build a 'flying machine', but if we look into Leonardo's notes we will find no such expression. What he wants to make is a bird that will fly, and once more there is an exultant tone in the master's famous prophecy that the bird *would* fly. It did not. And shortly afterward we find Leonardo lodging in the Vatican – at the time when Michelangelo and Raphael were there creating their most renowned works – quarrelling with a German mirror maker and fixing wings and a beard to a tame lizard in order to frighten his visitors. He made a dragon, but it was only a footnote to a Promethean life. The claim to be a creator, a maker of things, passed from the painter to the engineer – leaving to the artist only the small consolation of being a maker of dreams.
E. H. GOMBRICH, *Art and Illusion*, 1960

In *The Adoration* Leonardo has sacrificed one kind of logic, that of the perspective-minded Quattrocento, but he has replaced it with another. In no earlier picture are we so aware of the explicit functioning of intellect, or of a comparable range and complexity of ideas. It does not seem to be only an accident of survival that we have, for *The Adoration*, so considerable an evidence of its preparation in drawing, and that these drawings are invariably concerned less with documenting a representation than with the working out of an idea. Not only is the style of *The Adoration* 'ideal' in the commonly accepted meaning for us of the word; it is the most ideated picture so far created in the history of art. Later in his career, when Leonardo had fixed his habit of recording ideas in words as well as in their visual symbols he defined in his own written language, most of the conceptions on which his new style was based. Often it is not in his explicitly artistic writings that a definition of artistic principle occurs, but in his scientific notes; since, in Leonardo's view, knowledge was indivisible and painting the preferred instrument of its communication, his principles of science were principles of painting too. S. J. FREEDBERG, *Painting of the High Renaissance in Rome and Florence*, 1961

The same deliberately empirical attitude lies behind *The Virgin of the Rocks*. A wish to get to the heart of nature and know the secrets was perhaps Leonardo's main impetus in everything he did; and such interest as he had in painting might almost have been to set up rivals to nature, fusing all his knowledge of her into the creation of things super-natural. In *The Virgin of the Rocks* the laws are nature's but the final creation Leonardo's. And he here defies the natural in many ways that cut across previous artistic assumptions. The result is organic rather than intellectual. Other painters threw a deliberate schema over nature, seeing it in terms of conscious mingling, enriched by art, whereby buildings were allied to scenery, minor groups of figures enlivened background spaces, and objects were artistically re-arranged to mirror a cosmic order. This showed the artist's invention. Alberti wrote of a delightful grotto he had seen, an almost eighteenth-century construction of varied stones and shells, but Leonardo designs a grotto which is the more marvellous for seeming not human work at all. It appears the product of natural forces: the rocks ribbed and smoothed by the constant motion of water, present in the winding river but felt in the subaqueous light and as giving moisture for the plants – each recorded with botanical accuracy – that grow so thickly and yet are pallid.

It still seems a region untrodden by man, because the figures who kneel in the grotto have something of the same inevitable growing quality as the plants; they are no stranger in their setting, and there is no sense of their incongruity within it.
M. LEVEY, *Early Renaissance*, 1967

The paintings in colour

List of plates

In the captions below the colour plates the actual size of the painting or of the detail reproduced is indicated in centimetres.

PLATE I   THE BAPTISM OF CHRIST Florence, Uffizi
Detail (54 cm.)

PLATE II   THE BAPTISM OF CHRIST Florence, Uffizi
Detail (life size)

PLATE III THE BAPTISM OF CHRIST Florence, Uffizi
Detail (life size)

PLATE IV   MADONNA WITH A VASE OF FLOWERS   Munich, Alte Pinakothek
(47 cm.)

PLATE V   MADONNA WITH A VASE OF FLOWERS   Munich, Alte Pinakothek
Detail (life size)

PLATE VI   MADONNA WITH A VASE OF FLOWERS   Munich, Alte Pinakothek
Detail (25 cm.)

PLATE VII MADONNA WITH A VASE OF FLOWERS Munich, Alte Pinakothek
Details (each life size)

PLATES VIII-IX   THE ANNUNCIATION Florence, Uffizi
(217 cm.)

PLATE X   THE ANNUNCIATION Florence, Uffizi
Detail (life size)

PLATE XI   THE ANNUNCIATION Florence, Uffizi
Detail (life size)

PLATE XII   THE ANNUNCIATION   Florence, Uffizi
Detail (life size)

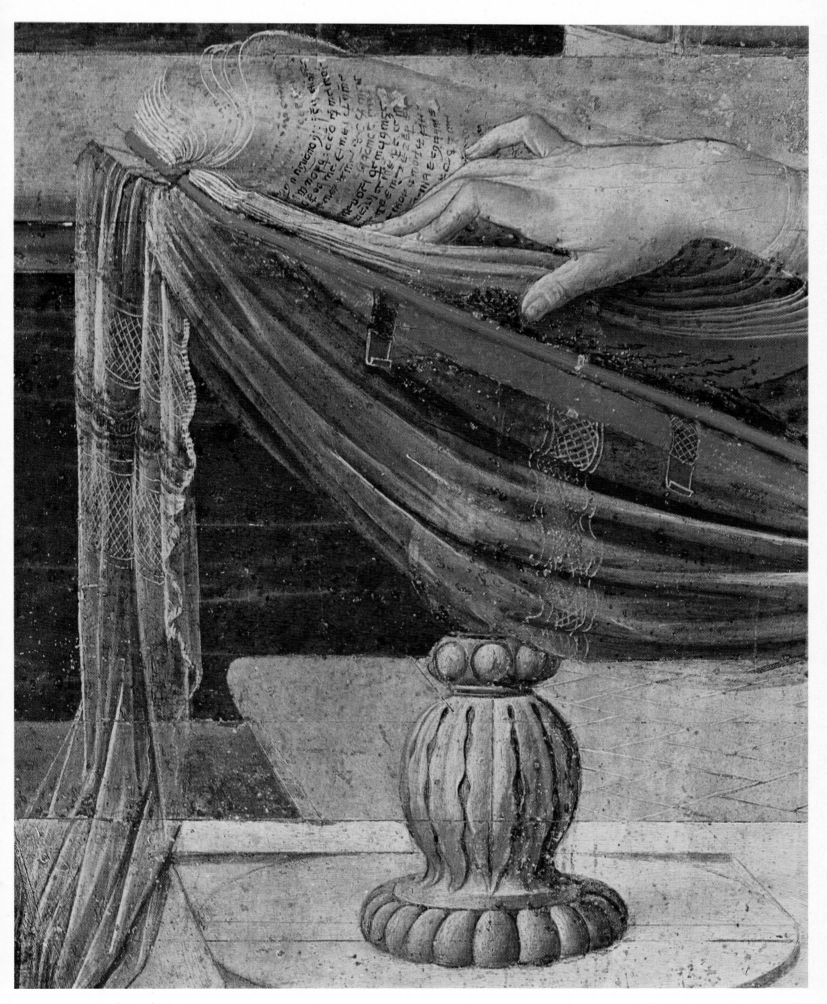

PLATE XIII THE ANNUNCIATION Florence, Uffizi
Detail (life size)

PLATE XIV   THE ANNUNCIATION Florence, Uffizi
Detail (life size)

PLATE XV   THE ANNUNCIATION Florence, Uffizi
Detail (life size)

PLATE XVI   THE ANNUNCIATION Paris, Louvre
(59 cm.) and detail (life size)

PLATE XVII   FEMALE PORTRAIT Washington, National Gallery
(37 cm.)

PLATE XVIII   FEMALE PORTRAIT Washington, National Gallery
Detail (life size)

PLATE XIX   THE ADORATION OF THE MAGI Florence, Uffizi
(246 cm.)

PLATE XX   THE ADORATION OF THE MAGI Florence, Uffizi
Detail (56 cm.)

PLATE XXI THE ADORATION OF THE MAGI Florence, Uffizi
Detail (56 cm.)

PLATE XXII   THE ADORATION OF THE MAGI Florence, Uffizi
Detail (56 cm.)

PLATE XXIII   THE ADORATION OF THE MAGI Florence, Uffizi
Detail (56 cm.)

PLATE XXIV   THE ADORATION OF THE MAGI Florence, Uffizi
Detail (life size)

PLATE XXV   ST JEROME Rome, Pinacoteca Vaticana
(75 cm.)

PLATE XXVI   ST JEROME Rome, Pinacoteca Vaticana
Detail (42 cm.)

PLATE XXVII   THE VIRGIN OF THE ROCKS   Paris, Louvre
(123 cm.)

PLATES XXVIII-XXIX THE VIRGIN OF THE ROCKS Paris, Louvre
Detail (78 cm.)

PLATE XXX   THE VIRGIN OF THE ROCKS Paris, Louvre
Detail (36 cm.)

PLATE XXXI   THE VIRGIN OF THE ROCKS Paris, Louvre
Detail (36 cm.)

PLATE XXXII   THE VIRGIN OF THE ROCKS   Paris, Louvre
Detail (36 cm.)

PLATE XXXIII   THE VIRGIN OF THE ROCKS Paris, Louvre
Detail (36 cm.)

PLATE XXXIV   THE VIRGIN OF THE ROCKS   Paris, Louvre
Detail (36 cm.)

PLATE XXXV   THE VIRGIN OF THE ROCKS London, National Gallery
(120 cm.)

PLATE XXXVI   THE VIRGIN OF THE ROCKS London, National Gallery
Detail (63 cm.)

PLATE XXXVII   THE LADY WITH THE ERMINE Cracow, Czartoryski Museum
(39 cm.)

PLATE XXXVIII   THE LADY WITH THE ERMINE Cracow, Czartoryski Museum
Detail (life size)

PLATE XXXIX   PORTRAIT OF ISABELLA D'ESTE Paris, Louvre
Detail (40 cm.)

PLATES XL-XLI   THE LAST SUPPER Milan, Convent of Sta Maria delle Grazie
(880 cm.)

PLATE XLII   THE LAST SUPPER   Milan, Convent of Sta Maria delle Grazie
Detail (73 cm.)

PLATE XLIII   THE LAST SUPPER   Milan, Convent of Sta Maria delle Grazie
Detail (46 cm.)

PLATE XLIV   THE LAST SUPPER Milan, Convent of Sta Maria delle Grazie
Detail (103 cm.)

PLATE XLVI   THE LAST SUPPER Milan, Convent of Sta Maria delle Grazie
Detail (73 cm.)

PLATE XLVII   MONA LISA   Paris, Louvre
(53 cm.)

PLATE XLVIII   MONA LISA Paris, Louvre
Detail (29 cm.)

PLATE XLIX   MONA LISA   Paris, Louvre
Detail (29 cm.)

PLATE L   ST ANNE, THE VIRGIN, THE INFANT CHRIST AND THE YOUNG ST JOHN   London, National Gallery
(101 cm.)

PLATE LI   ST ANNE, THE VIRGIN, THE INFANT CHRIST AND THE YOUNG ST JOHN London, National Gallery
Detail (life size)

PLATES LII-LIII   ST ANNE, THE VIRGIN, THE INFANT CHRIST AND THE YOUNG ST JOHN   London, National Gallery
Detail (life size)

PLATE LIV   ST ANNE, THE VIRGIN, THE INFANT CHRIST AND THE YOUNG ST JOHN London, National Gallery
Detail (life size)

PLATE LV   ST ANNE, THE VIRGIN AND THE INFANT CHRIST WITH A LAMB   Paris, Louvre
(112 cm.)

PLATE LVI   ST ANNE, THE VIRGIN AND THE INFANT CHRIST WITH A LAMB Paris, Louvre
Detail (40 cm.)

PLATE LVII   ST ANNE, THE VIRGIN AND THE INFANT CHRIST WITH A LAMB Paris, Louvre
Detail (40 cm.)

PLATE LVIII   ST ANNE, THE VIRGIN AND THE INFANT CHRIST WITH A LAMB Paris, Louvre
Detail (40 cm.)

PLATE LIX ST ANNE, THE VIRGIN AND THE INFANT CHRIST WITH A LAMB Paris, Louvre
Detail (40 cm.)

PLATE LX   ST JOHN THE BAPTIST Paris, Louvre
(57 cm.)

PLATE LXI LA BELLE FERRONNIÈRE Paris, Louvre
(44 cm.)

PLATE LXII   PORTRAIT OF A MUSICIAN Milan, Pinacoteca Ambrosiana
(31 cm.)

PLATE LXIII   PORTRAIT OF A LADY Milan, Pinacoteca Ambrosiana
(34 cm.)

PLATE LXIV   BACCHUS Paris, Louvre
(115 cm.)

The works

Key to symbols used

To allow the reader to see at one glance the essential elements of each work, the heading of each notice bears, after the number of the painting (which follows the most reliable chronological order and to which reference is made every time the work is mentioned in the course of this volume), a series of symbols relating to : 1) the execution of the work, i.e. its degree of authenticity ; 2) the technique ; 3) the support ; 4) the location ; 5) other known facts : whether the work is signed, dated, whether it is now complete with all its parts or whether it was ever finished. The other numbers appearing in the notice refer : the one above, to the size of the work in centimetres (height and width), the one underneath, to its date ; when such dates cannot be given with certainty, but only approximatively, they are preceded or followed by a star *, according to whether the doubt concerns the period before or after the date given, or both. All this information is in accordance with the prevalent opinion of contemporary art historians : all outstanding dis-agreements or further precisions are given in the text.

Authenticity

▦ Own hand

▨ With assistants

▦ In collaboration

▦ With extensive collaboration

▦ Workshop

▦ Generally accepted attribution

▦ Generally not attributed

Abbreviations

A : L'Arte (Rome – Turin – Milan)
AAL : Atti dell' Accademia Nazionale dei Lincei (Rome)
AAP : Atti dell' Accademia Pontaniana (Naples)
ADA : L'Amour de l'art (Paris)
AL : Arte lombarda (Milan)
AMM : Atti e memorie della R. Deputazione di storia patria di Modena (Modena)
AS : Arte e storia (Florence)
ASA : Archivio storico dell'arte (Rome)
ASI : Archivio storico italiano (Florence)
ASL : Archivio storico lombardo (Milan)
BA : Bollettino d'arte (Rome)
BM : The Burlington Magazine (London)
BSS : Bollettino storico della Svizzera italiana (Bellinzona)
C : Der Cicerone (Leipzig)
CA : La critica d'arte (Florence)
C. Atl. : Codex Atlanticus (Milan, Biblioteca Ambrosiana), manuscript by Leonardo, edited by G. Piumati [Milan 1894–1904]
CO : Commentari (Florence)
Cod. Arundel : Arundel Codex 263 (London, British Museum), manuscript by Leonardo, edited by the Commissione Vinciana [Rome 1923–30]
Cod. B : Codex B (Paris, Institut de France), manuscript by Leonardo, edited by C. Ravaisson-Mollier [Les

▨ Traditional attribution

▨ Recent attribution

Technique

⊗ Oil

⊛ Fresco

⊛ Tempera

Support

⊗ Panel

⊗ Wall

⊗ Canvas

Location

⦙ Accessible to the public

⦙ Private collection

⦙ Location unknown

⦙ Lost work

Other Information

▤ Signed work

▤ Dated work

▤ Incomplete work or fragment

▤ Unfinished work

▦ ⊗ ▤

Information provided in the text.

Manuscrits de Léonard de Vinci de la Bibliothèque de l'Institut de France, Paris 1881–91] together with various other manuscripts in the same institute
Cod. C : Codex C, manuscript in the same series as the one above and published together
Cod. E : Codex E, as above
Cod. F : Codex F, as above
Cod. Forster : Forster Codex I–III (London, Victoria and Albert Museum), manuscript by Leonardo, edited by the Commissione Vinciana [Rome 1930–6]
Cod. G : Codex G, manuscript in the same series as Cod. B (see above)
Cod. L : Codex L, as above
Cod. I and II : notebooks on anatomy (Windsor Castle, Royal Library), which are part of a series of four manuscripts by Leonardo, published by various authors, among whom K. Clark [A Catalogue of the Drawings of Leonardo ... at Windsor Castle, Cambridge 1935]
E : Emporium (Bergamo)
FL : La fiera letteraria (Rome)
GBA : Gazette des Beaux Arts (Paris)
GM : Gazzetta di Milano (Milan)
GSAT : Giornale storico degli archivi toscani (Florence)
GSL : Giornale della letteratura italiana (Turin)
JA : Jardin des Arts (Paris)
JPK : Jahrbuch der preussischen

Bibliography

The enormous literature on Leonardo has been listed in the Raccolta Vinciana, (Milan 1905–64), the Bibliografia Vinciana by E. Verga, (Bologna 1931), and the Catalogue of the Elmer Belt Library of Vinciana edited by K. Steinitz, (Los Angeles 1946 and 1955). The following brief list names only the most important publications of Leonardo's own writings and outstanding monographs published in English.
Leonardo's writings: E. McCurdy (The Notebooks of Leonardo da Vinci, London 1939); A. P. McMahon (Treatise on Painting by Leonardo da Vinci, Princeton 1956); C. Pedretti (Leonardo da Vinci on Painting, London 1965); J. P. Richter (The Literary Works of Leonardo da Vinci, 2nd edition, London 1939, reprinted 1970); I. A. Richter (A Comparison of the Arts by Leonardo da Vinci, Oxford 1949); L. Reti (The Madrid Codices, New York and London 1974 (facsimile, English translation and commentary)).
Select monographs: K. Clark (Leonardo da Vinci, London 1952, Penguin edition 1958); S. Freud (Leonardo da Vinci. A Psychosexual Study of an Infantile Reminiscence, translated by A. A. Brill with a Preface by E. Jones, London 1932); L. Goldscheider (Leonardo da Vinci, London 1952); C. Gould (Leonardo. The Artist and the Non Artist, Boston and London 1975); L. H. Heydenreich (Leonardo da Vinci, New York 1952); M. Kemp (Leonardo da Vinci. The Marvellous Works of Nature and Man, London 1981, with bibliography); E. Panofsky (The Codex Huygens and Leonardo da Vinci's Art Theory, London 1940); A. E. Popham (The Drawings of Leonardo da Vinci, London 1946); K. W. G. Posner (Leonardo and Central Italian Art 1515–1550, New York 1974); J. Roberts and C. Pedretti (Leonardo da Vinci. The Codex Hammer, formerly the Codex Leicester, Royal Academy, London 1981).

Kunstsammlungen (Berlin)
LA : L'Artiste (Paris)
PA : Paragone (Florence)
PR : Proporzioni (Florence)
RA : Rassegna d'arte (Milan)
RE : Revue d'esthétique (Paris)
RK : Repertorium für Kunstwissenschaft (Berlin-Leipzig)
RV : Raccolta vinciana (Milan)
ZBK : Zeitschrift für bildende Kunst (Leipzig)

Outline biography

1452 Leonardo was born in Vinci on 15 April, the natural son of Ser Piero di Antonio and Caterina, who later married Acattabriga di Piero del Vacca. A precise entry by Antonio da Vinci, 'My grandson, son of my son Ser Piero, was born on Saturday 15th, at the third hour of the night [corresponding to our 10 30 PM]. He was given the name of Leonardo. He was baptized by the priest Piero di Bartolomeo da Vinci', confirms the dates given on the tax return of Vinci for 1457: 'a dwelling house situated in the parish of Sta Croce [the church where Leonardo was baptized, on the Sunday in Albis] in the urban district of Vinci . . . Members of household: Antonio (myself), eighty-five years of age, Monna Lucia, my wife, sixty-four; Ser Piero, my son, thirty; Francesco, my son . . .; Albiera, wife of the said Ser Piero, my daughter-in-law, twenty-one; Leonardo, illegitimate son of the said Ser Piero and of Caterina, now wife of Acattabriga di Piero del Vacca from Vinci, aged five.' Leonardo's mother, coming from a 'good family' lived at Anchiano with her husband, on a farm belonging to Ser Piero. Bearing in mind that the tax return for 1457 was the first one made after the birth of Leonardo, it seems obvious that he was born not in Anchiano where his mother was to settle later, but in Vinci, in the house of his grandfather Antonio da Vinci, accepted by the family and baptized with some pomp. Which invalidates scientific theories, like Freud's, based on the kite dream ('in my very first memory of childhood, it seemed to me that, as I lay in my crib a kite came down to me and, with its tail, opened my mouth and hit my lips several times') and also poetic theories like Brion's, about the alleged desertion of the infant during the first years of its life.

1468 Antonio di Piero di Guido da Vinci, grandfather of Leonardo, died at the age of ninety-six, as shown on the 1469 tax return: 'sons and heirs of Antonio di Ser Piero di Ser Guido . . . Monna Lucia, wife of the deceased, aged seventy-four; Ser Piero, son of the deceased, aged forty; Francesco, son of the deceased, aged thirty-two; Francesca (daughter of Ser Giuliano di Lanfredini, married in 1465) wife of the above Ser Piero, aged twenty (his second wife); Alessandra, wife of the above Francesco, aged twenty-six; Leonardo, illegitimate son of the above Ser Piero, aged seventeen.'

1469 Piero and Francesco rented in the Via delle Prestanze in Florence (now Via dei Gondi), a house belonging to the Merchants' Guild (from 1465, Francesco was registered as a member of the Guild of Silk Merchants) and settled there with their respective families (the house was demolished later, when Giuliano da Sangallo built the Palazzo Gondi). In 1470, Ser Piero was Procurator of the Convent of the Santissima Annunziata, and then notary at the Signoria.

1469ca. Having grown up as the only son in his father's house (Ser Piero's first legitimate son was not born until 1476, from his third wife), Leonardo was apprenticed, presumably that year, in Verrocchio's workshop where he received a rigorous and complete training.

1472 Entry in the register of the Compagnia di San Luca in Florence: 'Anno Domini 1472 – Leonardo, son of Ser Piero da Vinci, painter, to pay the sum of 6 sol. for the whole month of June 1472, for the remittance of his debt to the Company until July 1472, and as an offering for the day of St Luke on 18 October 1472, 5 sol., and the same every year; to contribute 16 sol. every year for the upkeep of the company, and to pay for the whole of November 1472, 5 sol. due on 18 October 1472' (Florence, Accademia di Belle Arti, *Libro Rosso* A, 1472–1520, 93 v.). From the context of that entry (the register begins in 1472), it can be deduced that Leonardo had been a member of the company before 1472.

1473 5 August Date written by Leonardo on a landscape drawing (No. 8 in the Uffizi), his first dated work.

1476 8 April and 7 June Two anonymous denunciations were deposited in the 'Tamburo' against a certain Jacopo Saltarelli, aged seventeen, accused of sodomy with several persons, among others: 'Leonardo, son of Ser Piero da Vinci, residing with Andrea Verrocchio'. In the margin, the decision of the investigators: *absoluti cum conditione ut retumburentur*, an acquittal which, contrarily to Séailles' belief [*Leonardo* . . ., 1892], was not merely due to the fact that the accusation was anonymous.

1472–6 During that period, which corresponds to his employment in Verrocchio's workshop, Leonardo worked under his master and in collaboration with other assistants, on commissions such as the jousts organised by Lorenzo de' Medici in 1469 and by Giuliano in 1475 and the celebrations which marked the entry into Florence of Galeazzo Maria Sforza in 1471. Apart from the angel known to be by his hand in *The Baptism of Christ* (1), and first mentioned by Vasari, he painted a water-colour cartoon of *The Fall* for a tapestry which was to be woven in Flanders for the King of Portugal (the tapestry was never executed and the cartoon is mentioned as belonging to the Medici by the Anonimo Gaddiano and by Vasari), a shield with a *Dragon* for a farmer of Ser Piero da Vinci's, a *Madonna della Caraffa* once belonging to Pope Clement VII, a *Head of the Medusa* and an *Angel*, both the property of Cosimo I. Apart from those works, now lost, or whose attribution is in doubt or denied, Vasari records particularly interesting sketches such as a *Neptune on the Sea* and the portraits of Amerigo Vespucci and Captain Scaramuccia. From that period in Verrocchio's workshop date, without any doubt, *The Madonna with the Vase* (12), *The Benois Madonna* (9), and the *Annunciations* in the Uffizi and the Louvre whose attribution was once disputed (2 and 11).

1478 10 January After a meeting of the 'Signori e Collegi' Leonardo received a commission for the altarpiece in the Chapel of St Bernard in the Palazzo Vecchio. He received on account 25 florins on 16 March (10). This note in his own hand dates from that year: '. . . ember 1478, I began work on the two Virgin Maries' (Uffizi, fol. 446), one of which, according to Heydenreich, is probably *The Benois Madonna* (9).

1479 29 December Hanging of Bernardo di Bandino Baroncelli, murderer of Giuliano de' Medici, arrested in Constantinople and judged in Florence. There is a sketch of a hanging man with notes about the clothes (Bayonne, Musée Bonnat).

1480 According to the Anonimo Gaddiano, Leonardo 'lived as a young man in the house of Lorenzo il Magnifico de' Medici, who gave him commissions and made him work in the garden of the piazza San Marco in Florence'. Since Lorenzo only acquired the grounds in 1480, we must deduce [Chastel, 1964] that Leonardo, then almost thirty, was in the gardens not as a student, but as a sculptor employed on restoration and planning, as his master Verrocchio before him.

We see from the tax return of Ser Piero da Vinci: 'Members of household: Ser Piero, aged fifty-three; Margherita, wife of the above (daughter of Francesco di Jacopo di Guglielmo, his third wife, whom he married between her sixteenth and seventeenth year); Antonio, son of the above, aged four; Giuliano, son of the above, aged one'. Leonardo left Verrocchio's workshop about 1478 and lived away from home.

In March, he received a commission for the main altarpiece in the church of S. Donato a Scopeto, which he undertook to complete within the next twenty-four, or at most thirty months: it was *The Adoration of the Magi* (14).

1481 In the records of S. Donato a Scopeto (documents from S. Jacopo sopr'Arno, 1479–82) we find the terms of the contract and the payments made in connection with the above *Adoration*. He was also paid 'Lira 1, Soldi 6' in firewood for 'the painting of the clock'.

(Above) Detail from Tobias and the Three Archangels, from Verrocchio's workshop about 1470 (Florence, Uffizi). The head of St Michael may be a likeness of Leonardo at eighteen. Another presumed portrait of the young Leonardo, as David, the well-known bronze by Verrocchio (ca 1473, Florence, Bargello).

1482ca Leonardo left for Milan, leaving *The Adoration* unfinished. 'He began an altar-piece of the Adoration of the Magi, with many beautiful details, particularly the heads; this painting was in the house of Amerigo Benci, opposite the Loggia de' Peruzzi, and remained unfinished, like many of his works'; wrote Vasari, who went on mistakenly 'Gian Galeazzo, Duke of Milan, died and was replaced in the year 1494 by Ludovico Sforza who honoured Leonardo and took him to Milan'. This is a palpable error, for Gian Galeazzo was murdered in 1476 and Leonardo went to Milan in 1482 – which is also mentioned by the Anonimo Gaddiano: 'He was thirty years old when he was sent by Lorenzo il Magnifico to the Duke of Milan, to present him with a lyre, together with Atalante Migliorati who had a unique

Drawing (pen and ink with gouache and water-colour 196 × 280 mm.; Florence, Cabinet of the Uffizi, No. 8) showing on the recto a mountain landscape with a castle, on the left, and an open plain. In the top left hand corner, the inscription: 'On the day of Sta Maria della Neve, 5 August 1473', which establishes this drawing as the earliest dated work from the artist's hand. (Right) Drawing in the Musée Bonnat in Bayonne, connected with the hanging (1479) of Bernardo Baroncelli, the murderer of Giuliano de' Medici. Its authenticity has been disputed.

(Above) Drawing (red chalk, 333 × 213 mm.; Turin, Biblioteca Reale, No. 15741) generally accepted as original and usually believed to be a self-portrait, although we are surprised to see Leonardo, in about 1512, looking already so old (but it is a well-known fact that he looked older than his age). Presumed self-portrait in The Adoration *at the Uffizi (14).* Bust of an old man *(pen and ink sketch, 100 × 95 mm.; Amsterdam, Fodor Museum), probably a study for the above-mentioned* Adoration *and sometimes considered as a self-portrait. (Below) Sketch (Milan, Pinacoteca Ambrosiana) once considered original, but now rejected by most critics. Probably a portrait of Leonardo.*

LEONARDO · VINCI ·

talent for playing that instrument'. It is likely that Leonardo had already been in direct contact, at least occasionally, with Lodovico il Moro when the latter paid a visit of condolence to Lorenzo de' Medici after the murder of Giuliano, in April 1478, and Leonardo's main motive in going to Milan was certainly the equestrian monument of the Sforza. This is confirmed by the well-known letter to Lodovico il Moro offering his services (*C.Atl.* c. 270 r.) first published by Amoretti [1804]; it was probably written not in Florence but in Milan, since it looks like a memorandum established after the first meetings or talks with the duke and the 'bronze horse' is definitely mentioned. On the other hand, if we remember that *The Adoration of the Magi*, begun in March 1482, was left in a state indicating that the work was continued until the end of that year, whilst the contract for *The Virgin of the Rocks* (15) presupposes in its turn a period of settled life, it can be argued that the arrival of Leonardo in Milan took place between the spring and summer of 1482. One of the motives for his leaving Florence may have been the omission of his name on the list of the Florentine painters suggested for the decoration of the Sistine Chapel, which, however, might be explained by his slow working. It is also probable that, during his first stay in Milan, Leonardo may have painted either *The Musician* (25) or *The Lady with the Ermine* (27) which would account for the contract for the altarpiece in S. Francesco Grande (*The Virgin of the Rocks*) in which, he is called, with a subtle distinction, 'Maestro' and placed in front of his collaborators (Cf. **1483**).

1483 25 April Contract between the painters Leonardo da Vinci, Evangelista and Giovanni Ambrogio de Predis, on one side, and on the other side the Prior Bartolomeo Scorlione, Giovanni Antonio Sant' Angelo and other members of the Confraternity of the Immaculate Conception, for the execution of an altarpiece to be placed on the altar of the chapel of the Confraternity in S. Francesco Grande in Milan. This is the first dated and authenticated document proving the presence of Leonardo there, and for *The Virgin of the Rocks* (15).

The first sketches for the equestrian statue of Francesco Sforza, 'the Horse', probably date also from 1483, if we are to believe Baldassare Castiglione's claim that Leonardo worked on it for sixteen years [*The Courtier*, 1528].

1485 13 April If the 'best painter who, from the examples of his work I have seen, has no equal', mentioned in a letter from A. Terzaghi to Maffeo di Treviglio, ambassador of the Grand Duke in Buda [*Monumenta Hungaricae*

Historiae, 1877] is – as is most probable – Leonardo, he received from the duke a commission for a *Madonna* to be sent as a gift to Matthias Corvinus, King of Hungary.

1487–8 Payments made to Leonardo for the design, and to Bernardino de' Madiis or de' Abiate (Bernardino Maggi di Abbiategrasso) for the model of the cupola of Milan Cathedral (Milan, Archives of the Cathedral Workshop, *Liber albus*, 263; *Liber mandatorum*, Nos. 33, 37, 38, 42, 43, 62). Related sketches (cf *ca* 1482, and *C. Atl.* 270 r.).

1489 Between January and February, he designed a portico covered with foliage which fits the descriptions given by Calco and Dolcino of the temporary decorations for

(Left) Drawing by Michelangelo, about 1503 (London, British Museum) which used to be considered as a portrait of Leonardo but in which recent critics now see a scholar studying a sphere. Another presumed portrait of Leonardo, in the guise of Plato, in the fresco of The School of Athens *painted by Raphael in the Stanza della Segnatura in the Vatican (1509–11): the identification has been taken up again by recent scholars, such as Chastel, who believes it may reproduce an idealized portrait as conceived by Leonardo himself. Some have also tried to find Leonardo's features in the King David of* The Disputà, *in the same room at the Vatican, because of the similarity with the features of the Plato on the opposite wall, but that is unlikely.*

the wedding of Gian Galeazzo Sforza and Isabella of Aragon. Leonardo must have taken part in the preparations, which were interrupted by the death of Hippolyta of Aragon, mother of the bride (*Cod. B* 28 v., 54 v., 78 v. [ASL 1916]). According to notes dated 2 April, 10 and 17 May, Leonardo was busy with a book on the human figure.

On 22 July, Pietro Alamanni wrote from Milan to Lorenzo il Magnifico that Lodovico il Moro was asking for 'one or two artists capable of such work [the bronze horse] for although that work was entrusted to Leonardo da Vinci, he does not seem to me able to accomplish it' (Florence, State Archives, Medici correspondence [Müller-Walde, 1897]). This may allude to the search for bronze founders, who were a necessary help even to professional sculptors.

1490 On 13 January the celebrations for the Sforza-Aragon wedding were resumed at Milan castle, with the feast of Paradise : 'a representation of Paradise had been designed by the great ingenuity and art of the Florentine master Leonardo da Vinci, with the seven planets rotating, the planets being represented by men'

[Bellincioni, *Rime*, 1493, 148 v.] Other accounts of the festivities can be found in the Biblioteca Estense in Modena (*Cod. Ital.* 521 [Solmi, ASL 1904]). Instructions by Leonardo about the distribution and circulation of guests in a room (*C. Atl.* 214 r. [Calvi, 1916]) undoubtedly relate to those celebrations.

From 23 April the following autograph note : 'I began this book and started work again on the horse' (*Cod. C* 15 v. [Richter, I, 720]).

On 10 May Leonardo asked the makers of his model for the cupola of Milan Cathedral to repair the buttresses which were broken off and cracked ; on 17 May he received the settlement of the rest of his account (Milan, Archives of the Cathedral Workshop *Ordinazioni* 1466–90 *Liber mandatorum,* 1490).

On 8 June following a request

from the committee in charge of the construction of Pavia Cathedral, Lodovico il Moro ordered Calco, the duke's secretary, to send to Pavia 'that engineer from Siena' (Francesco di Giorgio Martini), and the 'masters' Leonardo and Antonio Amadeo. On 21 June Leonardo and Francesco di Giorgio were together in Pavia, as is shown by a bill for 20 *Lire* for expenses at the Locanda del Moro (Milan State Archives, *Carteggio Sforzesco* [Motta, BSS 1884]; Pavia, Register of the Cathedral Workshop, 1488).

1491 A note by Leonardo, dated 22–24 July : 'Jacomo came to stay with me on the day of St Mary Magdalen 1490, aged ten'. He was referring to Gian Giacomo Caproti from Oreno, known as *il Salai*, that is, the Devil, (a nickname he received from the *Morgante* of Pulci) who remained the master's disciple to his death. A series of thefts by the boy are recorded during the first eight months (*Cod. C* 15 v. [Richter, II]) ; from then on, year after year, Leonardo noted his expenses to feed, clothe his assistant and provide him with shoes. We are surprised by his indulgence with regard to the bad behaviour of the young man whose character Leonardo

defined from the beginning as 'thieving, lying, obstinate, glutton'. This did not prevent him from lending the boy thirty *scudi* (1508) as a dowry for a sister of his, from making a favourite of him to the end and leaving him on his death a considerable sum 'in return for his good and faithful service'. Which, taken in conjunction with the incident of 1476 (see above) and other more obscure episodes, gave rise to diverging interpretations, from the most severe condemnation [R. Keitler, *Internationale Zeitschrift für Psychoanalyse* 1916–17] to justification [G. Fumagalli, *Eros di Leonardo*, 1954], including a contribution by Freud [*Schriften zur angewandten Seelenkunde*, 1910]. A detailed criticism of those interpretations by R. S. Stites [*College Art Journal*

1948], leads to the acceptable conclusion that, in Florence, Leonardo 'certainly had the opportunity to come in contact with examples of homosexuality since the humanists praised the platonic love ideal found in friendships between men' ; however in all his works in the various subjects which interested him (including some of the most controversial – in that sense – of his anatomical designs), the master gave no absolute evidence of homosexuality. Apart from De Predis, Boltraffio also worked with Leonardo. We know that during that period, Leonardo and Gaffurio were in contact about the cupola of Milan Cathedral, for which Gaffurio engaged Fancelli in 1491. The epigrams by Francesco Arrigoni on 'the horse', written at the request of Lodovico il Moro, also date from that period.

An appeal from Leonardo and Ambrogio de Predis to Lodovico il Moro about *The Virgin of the Rocks* (15) dates either from that year or from 1492. Leonardo organised the preparations of the jousts given by Sanseverino, captain of the Sforza forces, to celebrate the wedding of Lodovico and Beatrice. He designed the costumes for the procession of Scythians and Tartars (Windsor) in Baldassare Taccone's *Danae* presented at the court in Milan in honour of Anna Sforza and Alfonso d'Este [Calvi, ASL 1916.].

1493 Leonardo visited Lake Como, the Valsassina, the Valtellina and the Val di Chiavenna ; he probably belonged for a time to the suite of Bianca Maria, wife of Maximilian, who was on her way to Germany. Leonardo was praised in verse by Bellicioni, Curzio and Taccone. He noted on 13 July : 'Caterina [his mother] came [to Milan] on 13 July 1493' [Richter, II].

1494 Improvements and restoration work at the Sforzesca, a model farm of the duke near Vigevano. [Richter, n. 1024–8]. Probably studies for *The Last Supper*.

1495 Beginning of *The Last Supper*. Also of the decorations of the *camerini* in the Castello Sforzesco, which were interrupted in 1496. Possibly dating from that year, a bill for the burial of his mother Caterina (Victoria and Albert Museum, *Cod. II*, 95 r.). Leonardo was mentioned among the duke's engineers [Calvi, III, 1869]. Plans for filling the moats of Milan castle date from that period.

1496 Beginning of the portrait of Lucrezia Crivelli, authenticated by epigrams of an anonymous author [Richter, II ; Uzielli, *Ricerche*, 1896] and by fragments of a letter from Leonardo to Lodovico il Moro in which he also alludes to work and money problems relating either to 'the horse', or to the decoration of the *camerini* of the Castello. (*C. Atl.* 335 v.).

1497 Sketches by Leonardo for allegorical compositions. Dated 29 June, a memoir from Lodovico il Moro to the Marquis of Stampa with instructions for Leonardo to finish *The Last Supper* and for the 'other wall' of the refectory [Cantù, ASL 1876] ; payments made to Leonardo for the said refectory [Amoretti, 1804]. About that time, sketches by Leonardo of the duchess's bath which he had devised [Amoretti ; Richter, 75 ; Calvi, ASL 1916] and a design for an altarpiece, later executed by Romanino, in S. Francesco, Brescia [Richter, I, 679].

1498 In the dedication to Lodovico of *De divina proportione* (8 February), Pacioli praised Leonardo who had completed *The Last Supper* and had also drawn some of the figures illustrating his own book ; moreover, he recorded the dimensions of 'the horse' and confirmed his continued relationship with Leonardo since 1496 and their scientific discussions which had taken place at the court. Between March and April, Gualtiero da Bascapè, a favourite of Lodovico's, reported to the duke the progress of the works in the Castello Sforzesco : the

Saletta Negra and the *Sala delle Asse* on which Leonardo and the duke's engineer Ambrogio Ferrari [Calvi, ASL 1916] were working. Letter from Isabella d'Este (26 April) and reply by Cecilia Gallerani Bergamini (29 April) in connection with the portrait of the latter painted by Leonardo [Uzielli, 1, 1896] (29). Leonardo was listed among the engineers of the household [Benadio, *Relazione storica*, 1711].

In a notarial deed dated 2 October the vineyard given by Lodovico il Moro to Leonardo, in the suburban district between the monasteries of the Grazie and of S. Vittore, is mentioned as neighbouring a piece of land which was changing hands (Milan, Archivio Stampa Sonchino). In the draft of an undated letter (but definitely from 1498) about the intended

1499 In May, Leonardo sent 600 gold florins to Florence, as a deposit with the Hospital of Sta Maria Nuova.

Lombardy was invaded by Louis XII ; Lodovico fled to Innsbruck and Leonardo left Milan with Pacioli. First he stayed in Vaprio with Melzi ; then he went to Venice, stopping on the way in Mantua where he was the guest of Isabella d'Este and executed two charcoal portraits of her (29). He may have paid a visit to Florence and Vinci, if we can date from that year an estimate of the movements of the hill of San Miniato and another of the statics of San Salvadore dell' Osservanza, which could however have been studied on drawings made by someone else, and finally a note about the conveying of household utensils to Vinci [Uzielli, *Ricerche*, I, 1884 ; Calvi, ASL 1916].

1500 In March, he was in Venice where Gusnago saw Isabella's portrait and wrote to her about it. In August, he was in Florence and sent to Francesco Malatesta, for the

Marquis of Mantua, the design of the house of the merchant Angelo del Tovaglia [Luzio, E 1900].

1501 With all his household, he was the guest of the Servites in Florence ; he designed the first cartoon for *St Anne* (30) and painted for Florimond Robertet, secretary of state of Louis XII, a *Madonna* now probably lost (32). The two works are mentioned in the correspondence of Pietro da Novellara with Isabella d'Este [Luzio, E 1900 ; Calvi, ASL 1916].

In September, Ercole I d'Este tried to buy the model of Leonardo's 'horse' which was in the Corte Vecchia in Milan and was 'deteriorating all over because nobody looked after it' (Ferrara, Archivo Palatino [Campori, ADM 1965]). In the Corte Vecchia, Leonardo worked

on the monumental statue of Francesco Sforza and tried out his flying models on the roof : (*C. Atl.* 361 v.)

1502 Following an exchange of letters (3–12 May) between Isabella and Francesco Malatesta, Leonardo gave an estimate for four precious vases in rock crystal, diaspore and agate for 940 ducats, inclusive (Mantua, State Archives).

He entered the service of Cesare Borgia as his Architect and Chief Engineer, and accompanied him to the Romagna : see his notes on Pesaro, Rimini, Cesena, Cesenatico, Piombino, Imola, Faenza, Forli, Forlimpopoli, Bertinoro and about the Lanone valley (*Cod. L.* 88 v., 6 r., 78 r., 46 and 36 r. [Beltrami, 1912 ; Calvi, *Introduction to the Leicester Cod.* 1919]). A pass for Leonardo by Cesare Borgia is dated from 17 August in Pavia and allowed him to inspect the fortresses in his states (Milan, Melzi Barbò Archives [Della Valle, 1791–8 ; Amoretti, 1804]).

1503 A petition (3 March) by Ambrogio de Predis to the King of France on the subject of *The Virgin of the Rocks* ; the king empowered the Praetor of Milan to settle the question.

Opposition (23 June) from the Confraternity (15).

From March to June, Leonardo was in Florence and, according to Vasari, he started work on *The Mona Lisa* and on *Leda* (31 and 34). On 24–6 July, he went to the siege of Pisa to study the possibility of diverting the Arno ; he sent an account of his visit to Francesco Guiducci and an expense account [Gaye, *Carteggio*, II, n. 62 ; Milanesi, ASI 1844 ; Richter, II, 229]. He had received in April the commission for *The Battle of Anghiari* (33). On 18 October he joined again the Compagnia di San Luca. On 24 he received, so he could work on the cartoons, the keys of the *Sala del Papa* in Sta Maria Novella. The theme of that work, the description of the battle and suggestions for the composition are probably

due to Niccolò Macchiavelli (*C. Atl.* 74 r. [Solmi, GSL 1909]).

1504 On 3 January, 28 February, 30 June, 30 August and 31 December there were various negotiations and payments from the Signori di Badia and later from the Operai of the Palazzo Vecchio, to refurnish the apartments of Leonardo and from Leonardo himself a list of his requirements for working on the cartoon of *The Battle of Anghiari* (see **1503**) : timber and ropes for a scaffolding with steps and various mechanical contraptions, paper, cartoons, white wax, white lead, whitewash, plaster, turpentine (Florence, State Archives [Gaye, *Carteggio*, II]). On 25 January Leonardo was asked to join the committee which decided on the placing of Michelangelo's *David* [Gaye ; Milanesi, *Epistolario Buonarroti*, 1875]. On 1 April he received the first monthly payment of 15 gold florins on account for the above cartoon, as agreed at a meeting which took place at the Signoria on 4 May. (Florence, State Archives, *Deliberazioni*, vol. 168, 40 v. [GSAT 1858 ; Frey, 1909]).

Between 24 and 27 May Isabella d'Este wrote a letter to Tovaglia and another to

Leonardo, to ask for an *Infant Christ*, about twelve years old, to be paid on his own terms. Leonardo promised to execute that work during the hours left free by his commission for the Signoria.

'On 9 July at seven my father Ser Piero da Vinci, notary at the Palazzo de Podestà, died : he was eighty years old and left ten sons and two daughters'.

Pomponio Gaurico mentioned (*De Sculptura*, 1504) Leonardo among the most famous artists.

1505 Through Luigi Ciocca, Salai, in Florence, offered to 'make something as a compliment to Isabella d'Este'.

Various payments, dated 28 February, 30 April, 30 August, 30 October for the building of the mobile scaffolding for the representation of *The Battle of*

(*Left*) Portraits of Leonardo on woodcuts published respectively in the second edition of G. Vasari's Lives (*Florence, 1568*), in the Opus chronographicum by P. Opmer (*Antwerp, 1611*) and in the Académie des Sciences et des Arts by I. Bullart (*Amsterdam, 1682*): obviously the last two (like various others which appeared in similar works, printed later) are derived from the first, cut for Vasari, which in turn may be derived from the profile in the Ambrosiana in Milan (see p. 84). The cap, which has become a typical element of the master's iconography (as we can see from a long series of modern representations: for instance the naive monument made by P. Magni in 1872 for the Piazza della Scala in Milan), may be connected with the plate (*Florence, Uffizi*) reproduced here on p. 86, or better with its possible prototype, now lost. The last portrait shown here probably also goes back to the sketch in the Ambrosiana; it may have been painted at the end of the sixteenth century, and is now at the Uffizi (*Reserve*) in Florence.

bronze doors of Piacenza cathedral, to the committee who supervised its construction, he alluded to his own experience as a bronze founder.

Anghiari (see **1504**), for various requirements in connection with that fresco, and for Leonardo's assistants.

On 1 April the Duke of Ferrara wanted to acquire a *Bacchus* painted by Leonardo, the property of Pallavicino who had already promised it to the Cardinal of Rouen (Modena, State Archives [distich by Giraldi ; Beltrami, 1919]).

On 30 April in Florence, '18.9.8 Lire' were paid on behalf of Leonardo as a 'duty on a parcel of his clothes sent from Rome' [Gaye, *Carteggio*, II] : from this, and from a temporary interruption of the monthly payment, Solmi deduced that Leonardo had gone to Rome, where his great friend Segni was a contractor for the Mint (the existence among Leonardo's papers of designs and advice for melting silver must be noted here).

A new manuscript (*Cod. Forster*) indicates 'begun by me, Leonardo da Vinci, on 12 July 1505'. Meanwhile, he was working on *The Battle of Anghiari*.

1506 The heirs of Evangelista de Predis sent (13 February) their uncle, Ambrogio, to represent them for the settling of accounts pending with the Confraternity of the Immaculate Conception ; the documents were signed on 4 and 27 April (15).

On 30 April the inheritance of Ser Piero was divided by the executors chosen by his widow. Leonardo was not among them, which would prove that he had never been legitimatised.

From 3 to 12 May an exchange of letters between Alessandro Amadori, brother of Ser Piero's first wife, and Isabella d'Este, about the small picture promised to her.

On the point of leaving for Milan where he was to stay from June 1506 to September 1507, Leonardo entered an agreement (30 May) with the Signoria to pay 150 gold florins as a guarantee to the almoner of Sta Maria Novella, if he did not return within three months. About the middle of the third month, on 18–19 August, Charles II of Chaumont,

(Left) Possible portrait of Leonardo in the fresco of The Marriage of the Virgin *painted by B. Luini about 1525 in the church in Saronno. – Panel acquired by the Uffizi in Florence at the time of the Lorena and entered in the inventory as a self-portrait of Leonardo. The doubts about its authenticity propounded by various scholars as early as the end of the nineteenth century were confirmed by radiography in 1938 which revealed, under the likeness of the master, a* Penitent Mary Magdalen, *dating from the seventeenth century. Therefore it is probably derived from the Turin drawing (p. 84), which however does not exclude the existence of a lost prototype (not necessarily by the master's hand) which Luini may also have known.*

Maréchal d'Amboise, Governor of the Duchy of Milan, and Goffredo Caroli, vice-chancellor, asked for a prolongation of one month, which the Signoria granted on 28 August, ready to free Leonardo from his commission on condition that he should pay the fine. Pier Soderini protested violently on 9 October, and on 16 December the Maréchal d'Amboise answered (the relevant documents, from the Florence State Archives, are reproduced in Gaye [II] and in Vasari-Milanesi [IV]).

Between that year and the following, Leonardo executed designs and gave estimates for the equestrian statue of Trivulzio (*C. Atl.* 170 v. [Gori, AAC 1881]).

1507 On 12 January Francesco Pandolfini, Florentine ambassador to the King of France, informed the Priors of the Signoria of the king's wish to keep Leonardo with him in Milan, and to commission from the artist some paintings and possibly his portrait. Louis XII wrote to the Signoria to that effect on 14 of that month, and on 22, the Signoria informed either

Leonardo or Pandolfini that the artist might place himself at the king's disposal.

On 27 April Leonardo was given back his vineyard of San Vittore, which had been confiscated.

On 26 July Louis XII asked the Signoria to resolve a question of inheritance between Leonardo, his court painter and engineer, and the artist's brothers. The letter is countersigned by Robertet: Obviously, by then, Leonardo had been freed from his Florentine obligations. For his case against his brother Giuliano (*C. Atl.* 342 v.) Leonardo appealed to Cardinal Ippolito d'Este [Campori, AMM 1865] on 18 September.

On 26 August in Milan, he received the first instalment due to him for *The Virgin of the Rocks* (25).

1508 Leonardo lived in Florence in the house of Piero Martelli where, on 22 March, he started on a notebook for mathematics and physics (*Cod. Arundel*). He worked on *St Anne* (35).

In September he was back in Milan (where he remained, apart from a few intervals, until the end of September 1513) and on 12, he started another manuscript (*Cod. F*).

In October, he lent 30 scudi to Salai to complete his sister's dowry and on 24 of that month, he ratified in front of a notary the final settlement of *The Virgin of the Rocks*, handed over on 23 to De Predis. He lived in his own house at the Porta Orientale, in the parish of S. Babila. Between July 1508 and April 1509 he received from the King of France a provision of 390 scudi and 200 francs (*C. Atl.* 192 v.).

1509 From that year date the geological and hydrographical studies of the valleys of Lombardy and of Lake Iseo. On 28 April Leonardo noted that on that day he resolved the quadrature of curvilinear planes (sheets in Windsor Castle [Müller-Walde, 1898]).

1510 On 3 March was established the agreement about the co-ownership of the dividing wall between Leonardo's vineyard at San Vittore in Milan and the neighbouring lands [Calvi, 1916]. On 21 October he met Amadeo, Cristoforo Solari and Fusina to discuss the stalls in the Cathedral (Milan, Archives of the Cathedral Workshop).

'This winter of 1510, I hope to complete all this branch of anatomy' (Windsor Castle, f.A, 2 v.): therefore his anatomical studies with Marcantonio della Torre at Pavia University must date from that year. From 1510–11, an undated rough copy of a letter replying to the official in charge of water supplies to obtain the 12 ounces of water allotted to him by the king from the canal of San Cristoforo. And he worked on two *Madonnas*, almost finished, one for the king, the other for the said official.

1511 He complained that Francesco (Melzi) did not answer his letters (*C. Atl.* 93 r., 317 r., 372 v.); those last notes are certainly from 1511, that is from Florence where Leonardo was staying because of his lawsuit against his brothers. But under the dates of 10 and 18 December he recorded that the Swiss had caused two fires in Milan (Windsor Castle [Richter, n. 1022]): it was the invasion of the Duchy by Massimiliano, son of Lodovico il Moro.

1512 Restoration of the Sforza by Massimiliano; it is not known exactly whether Leonardo was at Vaprio staying with Melzi, or what he was working on.

1513 On 25 March Leonardo was in Milan, the guest of Prevostino Viola (Milan, Archives of the Cathedral Workshop).

On 30 April a barrier was put up in the Great Council Room of the Palazzo Vecchio in Florence to protect the finished part of *The Battle of Anghiari* (33).

On 24 September Leonardo left Milan with Melzi, Salai, Lorenzo and Fanfoia (*Cod. E* 1 v. [Richter, n. 414]) for Rome, where he lived at the Belvedere in the Vatican in rooms specially prepared and furnished [Hoogewerff, CO 1952]. Under the patronage of Giuliano de' Medici, he worked for three years, until 1515, on mathematical and scientific research.

1514 He resided in Rome, with journeys (September) to Parma and Sant' Angelo, to Bologna and to Florence (*Cod. E* 80 v. [Richter, n. 1065; Amoretti]). In July, he was in Rome, where on 7 he completed a geometrical demonstration (*C. Atl.* 90 v.).

Probably from that year, a reference to one of his mathematical works on the quadrature of the circle and on curvilinear surfaces, and the beginning of his *De Ludo Geometrico* (*C. Atl.* 170 r. & 45 v.)

On 14 December he noted that Battista dell'Aquila had been given his manuscript *De Voce* (*C. Atl.* 287 r.).

Dating from 1514–15, studies on the draining of the Pontine Marshes (the project was approved by Leo X on 14 December 1514) and about the port of Civitavecchia [Solmi, ASL 1910], and *Leda*, painted, apparently, for Giuliano de' Medici (34).

1515 On 9 January Leonardo noted the departure from Rome of Giuliano de' Medici and the death of Louis XII (*Cod. G* [Richter, II, n. 417]).

1516 August He recorded the measurements of the basilica of S. Paolo, (*C. Atl.* 172 v.), which confirms his residence in Rome at that date.

1517 He accepted the hospitality offered by François I at the Château de Cloux, near

Other presumed portraits of Leonardo, (above). Marble relief possibly sixteenth-century Lombard (Milan, Castello Sforzesco). Terracotta (Aharon Collection, New York) previously believed to be by G. F. Rustici or the sixteenth-century Tuscan school, probably derived from the Ambrosiana profile (p. 84).

Detail of folio 283 (verso) of the Codex Atlanticus, representing the 'weary hand', that is to say, the left hand, of the master practising his left-handed writing.

Amboise, and was there in May, for the Feast of the Ascension (*C. Atl.* 103 r.). On the occasion of the welcome given to François I by the town of Argentan, there is a mention of a mechanical lion devised by the artist [Solmi, ASL 1904].

On 10 October Antonio de Beatis, (*Itinerario del Cardinale d'Aragona*) mentions a visit of the Cardinal of Aragon to Leonardo, 'over seventy years old', and names three paintings: the portrait of 'a certain Florentine lady', *St John the Baptist* and *St Anne* (31, 35 and 37), 'all most perfect; but it is true that since he is affected by a kind of paralysis of the right hand, no good work can be expected of him any more. There is a Milanese (Francesco Melzi) who works fairly well and although Leonardo can no longer handle colours with his previous subtlety, he can still draw and teach others.'

1518 Leonardo possibly took part either in the organizing of the May celebrations at Amboise for the christening of the Dauphin and for the wedding of Lorenzo de' Medici with a niece of the king's, or in those of June in Cloux in honour of François I, devising displays similar to those of the *Festa del Paradiso* in Milan in 1490.

From his own notes (*C. Atl.* 33 v., 336 v. and *Cod. Arundel D*, 221 r., 369 r.), we learn that he was studying the possibility of a canal for irrigation through Tours, Blois and the Saône.

During the last two years, he received in all a pension of ten thousand *scudi* (Paris, National Archives).

1519 On 23 April Leonardo made his last will and testament [Beltrami, *Documenti*, 1919 (from the copy in the Melzi Library; the original has been lost)], asking to be buried near the church of St Florentin in Amboise. His executor was Melzi, to whom he left all his manuscripts and 'the tools of his painter's craft', also what was still owed to him by the king's treasury, the money he had in the house, and his own clothes. He left his Milan vineyard half to Battista de Vilussis, his servant, half to Salai. He made bequests for his servant-maid, for the poor and for the churches of Amboise. To his brothers in Florence, he bequeathed an estate in Fiesole and the money deposited (400 *scudi* and the interest thereof) in Sta Maria Novella.

He died on 2 May; Melzi informed his brothers on 1 June, giving them at the same time the terms of the will which concerned them. On 12 August *fut inhumé dans le cloistre de cette église M. Lionard de Vincy, noble millanois et premier peintre et ingénieur et architecte du Roy, meschanischien d'estat et anchien directeur de peincture du duc de Milan* (Amboise, Register of the Royal Chapter of St Florentin [Hardouin, *Cabinet de l'amateur*, 1863]). His ashes were scattered during the wars of religion.

Catalogue of works

There are only four paintings by Leonardo whose attribution has never given rise to any controversies : *The Adoration of the Magi, St Jerome, The Last Supper* and *The Mona Lisa*. The first two are unfinished ; the third, miraculously kept as a skeleton of a composition with some traces of colour, has always been a shadow of its former self ; but *The Mona Lisa* is more or less intact. On the other hand, there are catalogues of the most diverse attributions. The first of them, in modern times, by Rigollot [1849] includes about ninety works. An even larger one is the *catalogue raisonné* by Müntz in his monograph of 1899. This enormous discrepancy is due, we think, to the fact that the artist's fame which was already great during his life, grew even more after his death, mainly for literary reasons : for centuries people talked of Leonardo and worshipped him, but without seeing his works. This situation, which is unique in the history of painting, is further complicated by the difficulty of making the works documented in the sources coincide with those attributed by critics, so that the two *Madonnas* of 1478, the portraits of *Cecilia Gallerani, Lucrezia Crivelli* and *Ginevra Benci* – to name only the best known examples – are without definite references.

An exact cataloguing of the works of the first Florentine period presents practically unsurmountable difficulties on which the most famous European scholars, and more recently American art historians, have laboured in vain for the last hundred years. Those difficulties derive from the constant exchange of ideas between philosophers, scholars and artists in Florence during the last thirty years of the century : a painting was often born from suggestions or in direct or indirect collaboration. But the situation is further complicated by Leonardo working in the workshop of Verrocchio, a many-sided and impressive genius, sculptor and goldsmith, painter and musician, and perhaps also architect. Great names appear among his assistants and pupils – Botticelli, Perugino, Leonardo, Lorenzo di Credi – and his connections with other workshops – from that of Pollaiuolo to that of Ghirlandaio – are numerous so that there is no single work out of that workshop which does not bear signs of collaboration. This complex round of influences and exchanges creates a labyrinth of possible hypotheses which will always lack a guiding thread, unless chance provides us one day with some artist's diaries or some legal documents to settle the game of attributions. This applies particularly to the young Leonardo, who arrived in Florence with a remarkable store of ideas and technical skill, and was Verrocchio's assistant for at least eight years.

From that first Florentine period, Vasari records the angel in *The Baptism*, the tapestry cartoon of *The Fall*, the dragon painted on a shield for a farmer of Ser Piero da Vinci, the *Head of the Medusa*, the bust of an *Angel* and *The Adoration of the Magi*. Leonardo himself mentions the two *Madonnas* begun at the end of 1478 ; and the commission of an altarpiece for the chapel of the Palazzo Vecchio is documented. *The Baptism* and *The Adoration of the Magi* have survived, and possibly copies of *The Angel* ; all the rest is lost and there is no reliable trace of the two *Madonnas*. Attributions, some controversial, include the two *Annunciations*, in the Uffizi and the Louvre, *The Benois Madonna, The Madonna with the Vase of Flowers, The Lady* once in the Liechtenstein Collection and – the only undisputed one – *St Jerome*. From *The Baptism* angel to *The Adoration of the Magi*, Leonardo's first period probably matured from the promise of *The Benois Madonna*, showing a development in the Louvre *Annunciation* and an acute analytical search in the Liechtenstein portrait and in *St Jerome* ; this last painting, with its intense feeling, announces in its turn the rich flowering of *The Adoration*, which is a high point of achievement through the profound renewal of iconography, and of composition, and the transmutation of a traditional legend into a universal myth.

Vasari describes Leonardo in Milan first as a musician, an improviser of verse, a thinker ; he then records a *Nativity* 'sent to the Emperor' and *The Last Supper* which he defines as : purely Milanese painting, nothing else. His silence over *The Virgin of the Rocks* is strange, since he should have seen the version now in London. He writes at length about 'the horse' (the Sforza monument), about the anatomy studies, the treatise on painting, about Melzi, whom he knew, and Salai ; but none the less Vasari's laconic brevity about twenty years of activity of a Tuscan (and no ordinary Tuscan) in Lombardy is surprising. Milanese documents or testimonies record *The Virgin of the Rocks*, the portraits of Cecilia Gallerani and Lucrezia Crivelli, the *Sala delle Asse* and the *Saletta Negra* in the Castello Sforzesco, and perhaps *The Madonna* for Matthias Corvinus. If we discard *The Nativity* for the Emperor, which one critic tried to identify without any foundation with *The Virgin of the Rocks*, and *The Madonna* for Matthias Corvinus, which is a pure critical hypothesis, however plausible, few works are documented : one of them the *Saletta Negra* has been destroyed, and another, the *Sala delle Asse*, has been completely restored. We are left with the first version of *The Virgin of the Rocks*, and *The Last Supper, The Madonna Litta* and four portraits : *The Musician, The Lady with the Pearl Hair-Net, The Lady with the Ermine*, and *The Belle Ferronnière*. Scholars have exhausted their imagination and their iconographic and historical research to try and fit those female portraits with the existing documents, debating not only whether the pictures are by Leonardo's hand, but whether this or that lady from the Milanese aristocracy is represented. But the real problem is only the former : for the creator of *The Adoration* and of *The Virgin of the Rocks*, none of those portraits represents an advance, neither the transparent ivory-like features of *The Musician*, nor the fine, calm, cameo profile of the Ambrosiana *Lady*, nor the lively, opulent *Belle Ferronnière* who has just drawn a deep breath. The only portrait worthy of his genius and of his inspiration remains *The Mona Lisa* : this inimitable creation is separated from the previous merely perfect portraits not by years of varied and divergent activities, but by worlds and centuries of pictorial art. However, this reasoning based on psychological and aesthetic data would tend to exclude all four contested portraits and it seems too much of a simplification to be valid. In Milan, Leonardo found a great art in a state of development : from the lunettes of the Portinari chapel to the frescoes of the Medici Bank he was faced with the beautiful works of Foppa, the landscapes of Bergognone and Braccesco, which opposed to the plastic principles of the Tuscan painters, to the Florentine and Verrocchiesque rhythm, the perspective, the light, the space of Lombardy. A different type of painting which, independently of Leonardo and before him, had tackled his own problems of light and shade, of distant horizons, of atmosphere, and which affected him to a certain extent, whilst being in its turn deeply influenced by him. Thus from the grafting of genius onto relatively coarse, but robust Lombard stock was born the Leonardo school (Boltraffio, Solario, Ambrogio de Predis, Cesare da Sesto, Melzi, Salai, Marco d'Oggiono) – which could only be born in Lombardy. During that Milan period, Leonardo's portrait painting was refined by his courtly surroundings, purified by Flemish influences, by the example of Antonio Pisano, and perhaps of Antonello, with infinite taste and balance. Leonardo may have attained that taste, that style, that formula for reasons of convenience and necessity, and developed the Lombard portrait to its extreme possibilities. A highly technical and spiritual creation, but not an autonomous, free product of his own genius. Thus are explained the portraits in this present catalogue (25, 26, 27 and 28) and we can say, without fear of great error, that perhaps none of them is entirely his work, but none of them is completely alien to him either. As for the two masterpieces which open and close the Milan period of Leonardo's painting, if we compare the Paris version of *The Virgin of the Rocks* with the Florence *Adoration of the Magi* which preceded it by a short time, we can see how much Lombardy with its humid atmosphere, its silvery light and cloudy skies, its sweet smell of earth, modified Leonardo's twilight lighting, that *sfumato* which models all outlines in subtle dark shades.

The few entries of Vasari for the various journeys undertaken over fifteen years, only record the artist's stays in Florence and in Rome, ignoring his other wanderings and the return to Milan before his leaving for France. The works mentioned are few, and hardly any were painted in Florence : the cartoon for *St Anne*, the *Portrait of Ginevra Benci, The Mona Lisa, The Battle of Anghiari* and two small pictures for Baldassare Turini. But, if the *Ginevra Benci* portrait is *The Lady* formerly in the Liechtenstein Collection, this picture belongs to the first Florentine period and the Turini pictures have disappeared. Whilst Leonardo alludes to two nearly completed *Madonnas* in a letter of 1508–10, other contemporary sources mention the cartoon of *Isabella d'Este, Leda*, of which there are several contemporary versions, as of *The Madonna with the Yarn Winder*. Only *Bacchus* and *St John the Baptist* are documented ; others are documented but lost, and among doubtful attributions are a *Pomona* and a 'small picture' for the King of France, a *Bacchus* the property of Antonio Maria Pallavicino and finally a *Medusa* once belonging to the Gonzaga family and various other altarpieces. Completing as much as possible a catalogue by Adolfo Venturi [1920] and a list by De Rinaldis [1926], we have mentioned in an appendix the most important works which have been assigned to Leonardo, from his own period to the last century. They show clearly the pitfalls which for centuries have lined the critics' path ; – the passion of collectors and scholars for finding traces of the famous artist, and also the very real difficulties created by the variations in Leonardo's manner ; all those factors, together with the blind compliance of the Leonardo school, have given less expert eyes the illusion of so many discoveries.

As for works from *St Anne* to *The Mona Lisa*, from *Isabella d'Este* to the lost *Leda* and to *St John the Baptist*, the recording in those short notes of prices and values without comparisons would have been an unnecessary addition to an age-old literature. Every one of us can discover for himself the incalculable value of each of those works which is a creation, a whole new world conjured up by a genius.

From what has been revealed by recent and accurate technical examinations [Hours, ADA 1953], which however did not succeed in resolving the mystery of some aspects of his characteristic modelling of light and shade, Leonardo began with a very fine white preparation : it consisted of a mixture of twice distilled turpentine, white lead, lime, (spirits), arsenic and corrosive sublimate ; this was covered with a mixture of varnish and whitewash then washed with urine and rubbed smooth with pumice stone. This was the 'greasy' priming ; occasionally, the master used a 'lean' priming, replacing oil by glue (a paste based on varnish, linseed oil, Naples yellow and whitewash). Over this priming.

1 Plates I-III

which was very hard as well as smooth, he spread a coat of reddish colouring, and started painting with blue, brown, red and white, in simple outlines and gradually the forms emerged – first indicated by thin traces of the brush – by means of superimposed dark and light shades, and gradually coming nearer to the aim he had fixed himself. It was substantially a technique of thin glazes akin to that used by the great Flemish painters of the fifteenth century ; by this technique he achieved a direct connection between the first touches and the last in so much as the latter were influenced by the former which he allowed to show through even in the finished work. The various layers of colour were covered with an oily varnish which was meant to increase the final 'translucent' quality. (That is why Leonardo's painting is called 'in oils' and we shall keep that terminology in the present catalogue. But in fact it is more a mixed technique including the types of media used in the typically mediaeval 'tempera' technique).
Therefore the pigments are 'in suspension' in an oily 'support' ; the result is so smooth and homogeneous that examinations in various kinds of light do not reveal a single trace of brushwork, leaving us in complete ignorance about the sort of touch used by the master.

1 ▦ ✇ 177×151 *1472-75 ▤ ⁝

The Baptism of Christ
Florence, Uffizi
Painted for the church of S. Salvi and attributed to Verrocchio in the *Libro di Antonio Billi* [1515]. From the Cloister of S. Salvi it was moved to that of the Vallumbrosan Sisterhood in Sta Verdiana, where it was found by the Arno department of the Commission for Works of Art and Science in Convents and was taken in 1810 to the Accademia di Belle Arti and transferred to the Uffizi

in 1914. Leonardo's contribution, consisting only of the angel in the foreground, is mentioned in Albertini's *Memoriale* [1510]: '... in Sancto Salvi most beautiful works, and an angel by Leonardo da Vinci' and confirmed by Vasari who combined the Billi and the Albertini traditions. The modelling of that angel in delicate shades was to influence all Florentine artists, as we can see from two miniatures from the famous Attavante workshop : the first, made between 1483 and 1485, shows a direct use of the group of two angels ; the second, from 1487, reproduced only Leonardo's angel [Chastel,

Art et Humanisme à Florence ..., 1959]. Vasari's confirmation both in the biography of Verrocchio and in that of Leonardo in the first edition [1550], repeated in turn by all historians, with the legendary tale of Verrocchio's discouragement and his supposed giving up of painting (which is false) through spite rather than envy, was not accepted by the first modern critics : Thiis [1909 and 1914] for instance, and before him Reymond [*Verrocchio*, 1906]. The attribution of the angel to Leonardo is no longer disputed.
A more recent, but also generally accepted, attribution is that of the piece of landscape behind the angel, with a large river between rocks, flowing from waterfall to waterfall and merging into the brightness of the background, one of the most personal lyrical creations in all painting, which an X-ray examination reveals as painted by Leonardo over a previous and different landscape [Sanpaolesi, in *Saggi e Ricerche*, 1954 ; Castelfranco, 1966]. The attribution originated with Bode [JPK 1882], who noticed that the tempera underpainting was, in the case of the angel, of Christ's hair and of the background, covered with an oil glaze. This famous essay was followed by the first critical study of the angel, by Seidlitz [1909], and the penetrating analysis by Guthman [1902], which added to Leonardo's oeuvre the whole landscape on the left. They were followed by Mc Curdy [1904 and 1928]. Recently,

Ragghianti [CA 1954], reconstructing with well-considered arguments the strange genesis of that work, has put forward the hypothesis that the picture came to Verrocchio's workshop about 1469, after having been begun by a minor artist ; it was first assigned to Botticini, then immediately afterwards to Botticelli and Leonardo, the latter being entrusted with the angel (1470), the landscape with the large valley on the right, painted in thin oil, as a transition between the deep, vibrating colours of the angel, and the figure of Christ which tends to a monochrome tone, with his shape highlighted by light and shade, and the landscape on the left, a sublime geological fantasy, which demands a comparison with sketch No. 8 from the Uffizi, with the autograph note : 'on the day of Sta Maria delle Neve – 5 August 1473', the first dated and uncontroverted work by Leonardo.

2 ▦ ✇ 104×217 *1472-75 ▤ ⁝

The Annunciation
Florence, Uffizi
This work comes from the church and convent of S. Bartolomeo di Monteoliveti, near Florence, either from the sacristy or the refectory, where it was traditionally attributed to Domenico Ghirlandaio. Vasari does not mention it. Transferred to the Uffizi in 1867, it was exhibited as a work by Leonardo on the definite advice of Liphart and appeared in the catalogue as such for the first time in 1869. Lübke [1870 and

1879] was the first to accept the attribution, followed by Bode [1882], Müller-Walde [1889] and others, among whom Venturi [1911], Berenson [1916], Siren [1916], Poggi [1919], Suida [1929] and, more recently, Clark [1939 and 1952], Goldscheider [1945], Castelfranco [1966]. The publishing by Colvin [1907] of a drawing of the angel's right sleeve indubitably by Leonardo (Oxford, Christ Church, A 31) was a decisive contribution to the Leonardo hypothesis. But in spite of this and other sketches, such as No. 2255 at the Louvre, a remarkable study for the Virgin's cloak, the ranks of the doubters were no less numerous, from Morelli [1883] and Cavalcaselle [1908], who put forward the name of Ridolfo Ghirlandaio, to Cruttwell [1904] and Reymond [1906] who chose Verrocchio, Frizzoni [1907] who thought the angel was by Leonardo and the Virgin by Lorenzo di Credi, Woermann [1905] and Seidlitz [1909] who denied Leonardo's authorship altogether. Among more recent objectors are Heydenreich [1931 and 1954], McCurdy, who backed the Verrocchio-Credi hypothesis, and Calvi [1936], who took up again the traditional attribution to Ghirlandaio.
In this age-long dispute, a scholar who is not a Leonardo specialist is struck at first sight by the variety of solutions suggested – all of them put forward by highly qualified connoisseurs of Florentine painting of that period. It shows first of all that the painting is devoid of any characteristic of composition or design likely to distinguish it clearly from other works of the period even the most famous : against Leonardo's authorship several other hypotheses, all founded on criticism valid or not according to the point of view, are offered. The compositional scheme had been common property for generations, with the angel on the left, the Virgin on the right, the lectern between them in the foreground as a relief done in perspective, the unavoidable architectural corner behind the Virgin's shoulders, the balustrade separating the peaceful terrace from a succession of receding planes with a remote view of water and distant mountains. All those were well-tried, pleasing devices, which we might almost call academic and of which at least two examples are known, by Domenico and his circle, in the mosaic lunette of the Porta della Mandorla of Sta Maria del Fiore and in that of the small church of the Orbatello hospital, not to mention drawing No. 287 of the Uffizi which uses exactly, with less room between the figures, the same composition as our picture. But the latter may have inspired the drawing, and not vice-versa. And the pictures just mentioned are later than 1480, whilst no relevant works by Domenico are known before that date. The dating of the

2 Plates VIII-XV

(From the left) preparatory study (red chalk, 85 × 95 mm.; Oxford, Christ Church) for the raised arm of the angel in 2. Study (brush, heightened with white, on canvas 260 × 225; Paris, Louvre) of drapery over legs, connected with the Virgin in the same painting.

picture in question to 1472–5, which is indisputable for Leonardo, would not be so for Ghirlandaio. If we concentrate on details, the angel, which is close to the angel of *The Baptism* (1), has attracted particular notice : the high forehead and the shock of curly hair which seems added, the radiance instead of a halo and the wings stylized according to the most traditional canons. Some critics believe that drawing No. A 31 in Oxford, of the sleeve, which is the most exquisite part of the figure, is more likely to be a refinement and a deeper study of folds derived from the painting itself, than a preparatory sketch. Radiographic examination has revealed a different initial scheme : the angel's head was more bowed and he was looking down. As for the Madonna, attention has been drawn to the cold expression of her beautiful face, the excessive rigidity of her neck and her small upright head ; it has been noticed that the left shoulder does not show under the hair and veil, that the two arms are out of proportion, and that the right hand and forearm cannot possibly reach with ease the book and lectern, since the latter, with its marble support, is aligned on the axis of the door. Her position with the knees apart, the academic treatment of the cloak are minor blemishes which may point to the first characteristic work of a twenty-year-old genius. It may seem strange that Leonardo, in a work all by his hand and finished should have been so conven-

Head of the Medusa (*Florence, Uffizi*), *dating from the seventeenth century and identified for a long time with 5, but already correctly listed in the Medici inventories as a Flemish work, possibly by Fr. Snyders* (1579–1657).

tional and so little original.

Against these pedantic remarks inspired by Morelli the picture stands out, luminous and fascinating in a mysterious way, with a chaste harmony which Domenico never attained, at least not alone and not to our knowledge. Looking at this 'Theocritus idyll' expressed through the light of dawn, with a fluid, brilliant surface which seems as if the paint had been mixed only with linseed oil, it does not seem too unlikely that it should be mainly by Leonardo's hand. Begun between 1472 and 1475, in Verrocchio's workshop, the outcome of collective ideas and contributions, and executed over a long time, intermittently, the

painting lacks the unity of a single creative impulse. This theory fits in with what we know of the slow, hesitating progress of Leonardo's work, driven here to its conclusion by youthful energy. The result is great stylistic and poetic nobility.

3 ⊞ ⊗ ⎯*1475 ▤ ⦂

The Dragon
Vasari alone mentions the anecdote of the peasant who gave his landlord Piero da Vinci a shield for his son to decorate. Leonardo painted on it a dragon coming out of its den and Piero sold it for a hundred ducats to some merchants who resold it for three hundred to the Duke of Milan. The details are so circumstantial that they do not seem to have been a complete invention of Vasari's. On the other hand, if we exclude confusion – made by some scholars with *The Medusa* in the Uffizi (see 5) which Vasari mentions separately, there is no other reference to *The Dragon* in Florence or in Milan, except by Bocchi who lists the 'horrible snake' painted by Leonardo in *Remarks on Donatello's St George* published in 1571 [Bottari-Ticozzi, *Lettere pittoriche* IV], but he certainly borrowed from Vasari.

4 ⊞ ⊗ ⎯*1475 ▤ ⦂

The Fall
This water-colour cartoon is mentioned by the Anonimo Gaddiano [1542–7] and described by Vasari. The work

was then the property of Ottaviano de' Medici. Leonardo's design, commissioned for a tapestry which was never executed (see Outline Biography 1472–6), was probably drawn immediately after *The Baptism* (1). There is no precise reference to the work in his writings or sketches. Suida's theory that Raphael might have been inspired by this cartoon has not been accepted by any other art historian.

5 ⊞ ⊗ ⎯*1475 ▤ ⦂

Head of the Medusa
Mentioned by the Anonimo Gaddiano [1542–7]: 'He painted a head of the Medusa

7 Plates XVII-XVIII

7 B

with strange and remarkable coils of snakes, which is now in the collection of His Excellency Duke Cosimo'. Listed in the inventory of 1533 or 1553 : and described by Vasari in the second edition of the *Lives* [1568], while it was at the Palazzo Vecchio in the collection of Cosimo I. The existence of the work is undoubted and it is difficult to understand how it was lost. It is even more difficult to understand how, from the end of the eighteenth century, on the basis of the Medici inventory of 1784 to the time of Milanesi [Vasari, IV], a Flemish picture should have been entered as by Leonardo. It is a work dating from the beginning of the seventeenth century, 'presented to his Excellency by the page Filippo de Vicq according to the will and testament of his uncle Ippolito de Vicq', and therefore must have been a gift to the Grand Duke Ferdinand II, about 1667. Leaving the documentation aside, a close examination of the picture should have been enough : the snakes are rendered in a typically Flemish technique and the foreshortening of the head is unworthy of Leonardo.

6 ⊞ ⊗ ⎯*1475 ▤ ⦂

Bust of an Angel
Described by Vasari as part of the collection of Cosimo I in the Palazzo Vecchio, and since lost. A late, badly cut-down copy of the work was sold to a dealer, with other rejects from the Medici gallery of the Uffizi ; it was bought by Luigi Fineschi who restored it and sold it to Prince Galitzin in Moscow, from whom it went to the Hermitage in 1888 (No. 1637), attributed to Giampietrino. The copy which belonged to Chéramy seems better. Since the original has been lost, we must be very cautious about the dating of the work. The pose ('the angel raising one arm, so that it is foreshortened from the shoulder to the elbow, and holding the other hand against his breast') corresponds to that of *St John* at the Louvre (37), which is probably Leonardo's last painting in France. In this case too, the complete disappearance of a work which

Vasari must certainly have seen more than once, is somewhat bewildering.

7 ⊞ ⊗ 42×37 ⎯*1474-76 ▤ ⦂

Portrait of a Lady (*Ginevra Benci* [?])
Washington, National Gallery of Art
On the front of the small panel, the portrait of a girl just out of adolescence, with strong features, stern and slightly mongoloid, against a background of landscape with water and plants dominated by a large conifer against the light. On the back (7 B) a sprig of juniper surrounded by a garland formed by a branch of bay tree and a palm tree ; a scroll with the motto *Virtutem forma decorat* links the three plants. This garland, a portion of which is cut off at the bottom, suggests that the picture has been cut down by a third (the sides were probably cut too, to maintain the proportions of a rectangle) and it has been surmised that the lower part of the bust, with the hands, had remained unfinished and was therefore taken off. Sketch No. 12558 at Windsor Castle might be a study for those very hands.

This small picture was in the collection of the Princes of Liechtenstein, in their palace in Vienna, without proper attribution when the great Waagen [*Die Kunstdenkmäler in Wien*, 1866] first put forward the hypothesis that this portrait of an unknown girl could be by Leonardo or alternatively by his best follower, Boltraffio. This controversy was resolved when Bode, in a monograph on Verrocchio [JPK 1882] and successively in 1892 and 1903 took up again Waagen's hypothesis, dismissing every doubt and identifying the portrait with Ginevra Benci, a Florentine lady born about 1457, daughter of Amerigo di Giovanni Benci, who at the age of seventeen, on 15 January 1474, married Luigi di Bernardo di Lapo Nicolini. Leonardo did paint Ginevra's portrait : the fact is mentioned by the *Libro di Antonio Billi* [1515], by the Anonimo Gaddiano [1542–7] ('he painted in Florence, from nature, Ginevra d'Amerigho

Benci, whom he represented so well that his work did not look like a portrait, but like Ginevra in person') and Vasari [1550 and 1568] ('He painted a most beautiful portrait of Ginevra d'Amerigo Benci'). These three testimonies are confirmed by the friendly relations which undoubtedly existed between Leonardo and the Benci family : when he left for Milan, Leonardo gave Amerigo the rough sketch for his *Adoration of the Magi* (14) and Giovanni is mentioned in autograph notes : 'my map of the world, which belongs to Giovanni Benci' (*C. Atl.* c. 130 r.), Nowadays the long controversy aiming at making that documentation fit the Liechtenstein portrait seems over, even though an obstacle to the identification is provided by Vasari himself, when he not only mentions the portrait as having been executed during the second Florentine period, but definitely places it at the time of the first cartoon for *St Anne* (30) which dates from 1501. The beautiful Ginevra was then over forty years old and could not have been the lady of the portrait. But we know that even Vasari can make mistakes. The attribution and naming of Waagen and Bode were accepted by Müller-Walde [1889], Strzygowski [1895], Suida [1903], Liphart [1912] and, in Italy, by Carotti, Beltrami, Schiaparelli, Malaguzzi-Valeri. They were rejected by no less famous scholars : Morelli [1893], Berenson [1896], Cruttwell [1904], Reymond [1905],

Reconstruction of 7B before it was cut, as suggested by J. Thiis [1909].

8   9

Thiis [1913], who suggested Verrocchio; Seidlitz [1909] supported the theory of the Florentine school; Poggi [1909], A. Venturi [1910] and Frizzoni [1911] assigned it to Lorenzo di Credi. After 1920, Berenson and A. Venturi accepted Leonardo's authorship for the painting, as have all well qualified specialists since.

The work is typical of the Florentine Quattrocento and Sir Kenneth Clark dates it from 1474. Castelfranco believes it

Virgin offering a Dish of Fruit to the Child (pen, 330 × 250 mm. Paris, Louvre), possibly connected with 9. (Below) Virgin and Child with a Cat (pen on a sheet of other sketches, 281 × 199; London, British Museum), connected either with 9 or 121.

B. Plants and Scroll
Verso of 7 A. (see above)

---

8   ▦ ⊕ 15·5 × 12·7 ▤ ⋮
              *1472-76

Madonna holding out a Pomegranate to the Child (Dreyfus Madonna) Washington, National Gallery of Art (Kress)
Until forty years ago this painting was considered

to be a few years later, whilst Nicco Fasola places it in the Milanese period, which would exclude Ginevra di Amerigo Benci and put the painting with other Lombard portraits; the modelling of the face has an indubitable resemblance with Verrocchio's marble Bust of a Lady (Florence, Bargello) and a certain family likeness with the Uffizi Annunciation Virgin (2) and the landscape has the same bluish tint as the background of The Baptism (1), the same Van Eyck-like transparency. Apart from the identification of the model, which after all, is secondary, in spite of the juniper, thanks to the documentary evidence and the research which followed the recent acquisition of the painting by the National Gallery in Washington, the attribution to Leonardo is now unanimous. It is difficult to find, in Verrocchio's circle, a painter capable of such fine understanding, such atmosphere, such modelling, and at the same time such a disturbingly impassive expression. A youthful work of the master — perhaps still in Verrocchio's workshop — would account for a certain relentless accuracy of modelling and draughtsmanship, a certain kinship with works by Verrocchio and his circle. The name of Ginevra, as a young bride, is obvious, even without the clue of the juniper behind her shoulders. We mention it only to answer Rosen who, in his famous Die Natur in der Kunst [1903], maintains that nobody has ever identified with any certainty the plant in the background of the picture.

one of the best works from Verrocchio's workshop and was attributed to Lorenzo di Credi. Suida [1929] was the first to attribute it to Leonardo, and was followed by Degenhart [RA 1932]. Those two critics thought that this Madonna, like The Benois Madonna and the Munich Madonna with the Vase of Flowers (9 and 12) showed the beginning of that blurring of colours, characteristic of his style. This picture is earlier than The Benois

11 Plate XVI
Madonna and has been dated between 1472 and 1476, whilst Leonardo was in Verrocchio's workshop. It could be contemporary with the lost Madonna with the Cat (121). There are no precise references to it among Leonardo's sketches and

Female Head (pen and wash heightened with white, 282 × 199 mm.; Florence, Uffizi) tentatively attributed to Leonardo as a possible study for the Virgin in 11.

identification is all the more difficult since the motif of the Child standing up on His Mother's lap is very common. Castelfranco still attributes the picture to Lorenzo di Credi; Baroni, Bottari and Goldscheider ignore the painting; more recently, J. Shearman [BM 1967] proposed again the attribution to Verrocchio already supported by Morelli but attacked by Passavant.

9   ▦ ⊕ 48 × 31 ▤ ⋮
         *1475-78

Madonna holding out a Flower to the Child (Madonna with the Flower; Benois Madonna) Leningrad, Hermitage. This picture was in the collection of Prince Kurakin, then belonged to the wife of the French painter Léon Benois who lived in St Petersburg. From Nicolas II, who bought it from her, it passed on to the Hermitage Museum (1914). The work came to public notice when it was shown without any attribution — together with other treasures from private Russian collections, in an exhibition organised by the journal Starye Gody. E. de Liphart [St Petersburg 1909, and Brussels 1910] categorically attributed it to Leonardo although he admitted that the painting had little charm and was unfinished; he noted for instance that, in the half-open

mouth, the teeth were only slightly drawn on the dark ground. After a few initial doubts, most art historians of the time accepted Liphart's attribution, with further studies waxing gradually more enthusiastic, so that the discovery took on a collective character and somewhat obscured the merit of Baron Liphart. Dissenting voices were few: Gronau [ZBK 1912] thought the picture might be a copy by Lorenzo di Credi of a Leonardo original from 1478, and Thiis [1914] found the painting undistinguished and attributed it to Sogliani, which attribution was accepted by Poggi. It is interesting to note that Berenson, who accepted the Leonardo attribution immediately, ruthlessly criticised the painting (a bald forehead, swollen cheeks, a toothless mouth, bleary eyes, and a wrinkled throat) and used it as an opportunity to reveal his dislike of Leonardo as a painter and to praise the essential, autonomous value of the drawings. Nobody nowadays doubts the authenticity of this Madonna which, through its elliptical composition and its modelling,

fits in perfectly with the compositional devices of the young Leonardo.
Brandi points out that the painting is based on an umber ground, over which the colours were spread 'in layers, like a dew', through a technique 'similar to that of the micrometric screw of a microscope, which gradually brings the object into focus' – a technique, in fact, appropriate to the 'deep, unfathomable quality which characterizes Leonardo's style'. Heydenreich [1958] dates the work from the end of Leonardo's Florentine period.

Critics believe that this work is the most likely to correspond to Leonardo's note '. . . ber 1478 began the two pictures of the Virgin Mary'. Among the master's early works, it is the most spontaneous and genuine. Unlike The Baptism (1), it poses no problems of adaptation of style since it is by one hand; unlike The Annunciation (2) it does not attempt elaborate compositional themes. Clark, following Colvin, connects it with sketch No. 100 in the British Museum and a beautiful study (No. 486) in the Louvre, of the Virgin holding out a plate of fruit to the Child which, on account of its draughtsmanship, certainly preceded the painting and therefore removes any doubt of Leonardo's authorship, because of its unfinished state. The painting is in a bad state of

preservation, damaged by being transferred to canvas, with overpainting on the draperies, mouth, neck and hand of the Virgin, the left knee and right hand of the Child and the background. But nonetheless this delightful girl-Madonna is one of the first and liveliest works of Leonardo; it inspired Raphael's lost Madonna with the Carnation and Lorenzo di Credi's Infant Christ in his Madonna No. 111 in the Sabauda Gallery in Turin, and it was copied many times. Gronau has made a close study of the copies, the best of which, in the Galleria Colonna in Rome, may be by Filippino Lippi. The work certainly remained in Florence until 1505–8, as we know from existing copies and variants. It has been hypothetically connected with a passage by Bocchi [Bellezze . . . di Firenze, 1591] in which he mentioned, in the house of Matteo and Giovanni Botti, 'a small oil painting of great beauty by the hand of Leonardo da Vinci, on which a Madonna is represented with utmost skill; the figure of the Infant Child is strikingly beautiful: he lifts up his face in a way most remarkable because of the difficulty of rendering that attitude with ease'. But this passage could apply equally well to the Munich *Madonna* (12).

10 ⊞ ✪  1478 ▤ ⁝
Altarpiece for the Chapel of St Bernard in the Palazzo Vecchio in Florence

On 24 December 1477 the Priors of the Signoria commissioned from Piero del Pollaiuolo an altarpiece for the chapel of the Palazzo Vecchio dedicated to St Bernard, to replace a previous altarpiece painted by Bernardo Daddi in 1355. Seventeen days later however, on 10 January 1478, they transferred the commission to Leonardo; the latter not only 'began to paint an altarpiece in the said Palazzo, which was later completed according to his design by Filippo di fra' Filippo', as we are told by the Anonimo Gaddiano, but was certainly paid 25 *Fiorini larghi*, on 16 March of the same year. The work, which was later left unfinished by Leonardo, was handed over to Domenico Ghirlandaio after a meeting on 15 May 1483, when Leonardo was already in Milan, and finally to Filippino Lippi, who finished it and dated it 1485. We know all this from the *Deliberazioni dei Signori e Collegi* (Florence State Archives). The document commissioning the work from Pollaiuolo seems to indicate that the Priors wanted an

12 Plates IV-VII

altarpiece representing the Virgin appearing to St Bernard – the subject of Daddi's painting – but Filippino's altarpiece (Uffizi) shows a Madonna enthroned between four saints, surrounded by architecture, and two angels flying above. On the other hand, the payment of 25 florins to Leonardo fits in perfectly with the statement of the Anonimo Gaddiano and we must postulate the existence of a cartoon by Leonardo. It may not

(*Above*) the main picture on the altarpiece in Pistoia Cathedral, the so-called Madonna di Piazza, *commissioned from Verrocchio and executed mainly by Lorenzo di Credi (1475–86).*
(*Below*) St Donatus and the Tax Collector, *from the predella of the same altarpiece (Art Museum, Worcèster, Mass.; attributed to Leonardo by Bayersdorfer, Valentiner, Suida and Langton Douglas, but not by other critics), to which 11 probably also belonged.*

have been finished, but it must have existed and must be listed with the lost works, even though no likely sketch has been found which could be connected with the commission. The hypothesis according to which the subject of this altarpiece was an Adoration of the Shepherds is rejected by Heydenreich [1954] as a tradition without any foundation, but is supported by Clark [1933]. Ragghianti suggests [CA 1954] that Lippi's picture might be based on Leonardo's conception (a theory supported by the invention of the angels in the apse of the background), and that traces of the original design might be found under this painting.

11 ⊞ ✪  14 × 59 *1478 ▤ ⁝
The Annunciation
Paris, Louvre

Part of a predella obtained by the Louvre in 1861 and ascribed to Domenico Ghirlandaio. Giovanni Morelli was the first to attribute it to Leonardo, in 1893, and his theory was accepted by all. The only dissenting voice was Goldscheider who, in a remarkable monograph [1952], attributed the painting to Credi, and tentatively suggested the possibility of a collaboration with Leonardo – which would not fit in with the unity of the work. More recent studies connect the painting with an altarpiece of the Virgin between St John and St Donato in Pistoia Cathedral, known as *The Madonna di Piazza*, commissioned from Verrocchio and almost unanimously attributed to Lorenzo di Credi, who might have worked on a design or sketch by Verrocchio, between 1478 and 1485. According to Valentiner's reconstruction [1950], the predella consisted of Leonardo's *Annunciation* in the centre, Perugino's *Birth of St John the Baptist* (Liverpool Art Gallery) on the left, and *St Donatus of Arezzo and the*

Tax Collector by Lorenzo di Credi (Worcester Art Museum) on the right.

In its details, this picture – later in date than the Florence *Annunciation* – is more coherent, more personal, more lively – so much so that Heydenreich tentatively admitted it in his catalogue of the master's works [1931], but excluded the Uffizi painting which, if we accept it as genuine, demands a complete change in our conception of Leonardo's youthful style and shows him restricted by formulae from which he seemed to have freed himself already then. To derive one *Annunciation* from the other would be absurd since their pictorial characteristics are mutually exclusive. Let us simply note that the microphotographs and X-ray executed in the Louvre laboratory reveal a hard, thick, white ground and numerous overpaintings. We must also remember that probably after Salvi [*Delle historie di Pistoia*, III, 1656], who attributed *The Madonna di Piazza* to Leonardo, the master's hand has also been detected by some in parts of the central painting [Valentiner, 1950; Clark, 1952; Suida, 1957]. This is extremely unlikely since, apart from anything else, *The Madonna*, whether or not a first draft already existed before, was only painted after Verrocchio had left for Venice and Leonardo for Milan.

12 ⊞ ✪ 62 × 47 *1478-80 ▤ ⁝
Madonna holding out a Carnation to the Child
(*Madonna del Garofano, Madonna with the Vase of Flowers*)
Munich, Alte Pinakothek

We know nothing of the story of the painting before its acquisition for the museum by Dr Haug of Günzburg in 1886. It was immediately exhibited as a work by Leonardo from his first Florentine period, probably on the advice of Bayersdorfer who identified it with *The Madonna della Caraffa* (Madonna with the Decanter) mentioned by Vasari in 1550 as belonging to Clement VII, then by Bode [1888], Fabriczy [ASA 1889], Geymuller [1890] and Koopmann [RK 1890]. Reymond, on the other hand [*Verrocchio*, 1906], denied the presence in the work of elements even indirectly derived from Leonardo and attributed it entirely to Verrocchio; Schmid [1893] assigned the painting to Lorenzo di Credi – but had no followers – and Morelli, followed by Rieffel [1891], Thiis [1909] and A. Venturi [1911], classified it as a copy or variant of a lost Leonardo original, by an unknown Flemish painter. But Venturi himself later proposed again the attribution to Leonardo [*Storia . . . 1925*], followed by Berenson, and, successively, Suida, Clark, Castelfranco, Heydenreich and many more recent specialists.

The painting is in a bad state of preservation, and the head of the Virgin and other parts were entirely repainted with a mixture too rich in oil, so that the resulting *craquelures* are different from those caused by the Italian technique and suggested to Morelli the hypothesis of a Flemish copy, like another picture in the Louvre, less beautiful, but well known in its time [Molinier, 1890]. Apart from the similarities between the Madonna in this picture and in the Uffizi *Annunciation* (2), including the rich folds of the draperies and the firm modelling of the hands, and apart from sketch No. 18965 in the Louvre – which Suida compares with the Madonna's head and which is certainly a variant of it – the originality of the composition and the determined attempt to obtain relief and monumentality differentiate this painting from those produced in Verrocchio's workshop.

Head of a Young Woman (*black chalk and brush, on pink ground, 225 × 265 mm.; Paris, Louvre*) *sometimes connected with the face of the Virgin in 12.*

(*Above*) poor copy of 12 (*Paris, Reserve of the Louvre*), *probably sixteenth-century Flemish.* (*Below*) *a derivation from the same painting (Leningrad, Hermitage).*

13 ⊞ ⊗ 103×75 1480* ▤ ⋮

St Jerome Rome, Pinacoteca Vaticana
There has never been the slightest doubt about Leonardo's authorship of this picture, from the moment it first entered art history, in spite of the complete absence of any testimony or documentation or possible connection with any of the sketches, in spite of its unfinished state (the painting has remained at the stage of a monochrome sketch), and in spite of its dramatic discovery. Once in the Vatican Museum, it was later acquired by Angelica Kauffmann, according to D'Achiardi, and was then lost and cut in two. Cardinal Fesch found the lower part in a Roman junk shop where it had been turned into a box lid and, years later, the upper part which his cobbler was using to wedge his bench. To accept that story, we have to believe that Napoleon's uncle perhaps knew the work before the engraving and publishing of the drawing by Gerli (Milan, 1784). In any case, Pius IV certainly bought the painting in 1845 for the Vatican Museum, and paid the cardinal's heirs 2500 francs for it. All the critics agree that the painting cannot be identical with another of the same subject attributed to Leonardo in the Palazzo del Giardino in Parma, since the measurements and the description in the 1680 inventory [Campori, *Raccolta di Cataloghi*, 1870] do not fit the Louvre picture. Heydenreich [1958] saw a hint of Pollaiuolo's style in the saint's tense, sinewy body. Most scholars agree to date the work from the first Florentine period, except Strzygowski [JPK 1895], who places it in the

14 Plates XIX–XXIV
first Milanese period, contemporary with *The Last Supper* (19).

14 ⊞ ⊗ 246×243 1481–82 ▤ ⋮

The Adoration of the Magi Florence, Uffizi
This work is at the stage of an underpainting in pale yellow and brown. In 1482 it was left in the care of Amerigo Benci by Leonardo, then leaving Florence for Milan, as we know from Vasari [1568] who mentions that the picture was 'once' in Amerigo's house (but no longer in his time). In 1621, it was in the Medici Collection in the Via Larga, and belonged successively to Antonio de' Medici, and to his son Giulio. After their death in 1670, it passed into the Medici Collection in the Uffizi and was listed in the 1704 and the 1753 inventories. Although the entries in the archives of the convent do not actually mention the title of the work, it is obviously the main altarpiece commissioned from Leonardo by the monks of S. Donato a Scopeto in March 1481, to be completed in twenty-four or at most thirty months. The artist never delivered it to them, and in 1496 they replaced it — as had happened in the case of the St Bernard chapel in the Palazzo Vecchio — by an altarpiece by Filippino Lippo with the same subject. This picture is also in the Uffizi now. The surviving preparatory drawings, which can all be dated to about 1481, confirm this theory, which is accepted by all critics, except Müntz and Strzygowski : the former claimed that the style was that of Leonardo around 1500, at the time of *The Virgin of the Rocks* (15), between the equestrian Sforza monument and *The Battle of Anghiari* (33) : the latter found the work too elevated for a beginner and the style too characteristic so, ignoring the evidence of the preparatory drawings, he invented a journey of Leonardo's from Milan to Florence about 1495 to account for the resemblance of Filippino's painting with that of Leonardo. Apart from other absurdities, the two famous critics forgot that in 1481, Leonardo was nearly twenty-nine and had behind him ten years of painting experience. We must cite here the article by G. Calvi [RV, X, 1919], which contains the most complete analysis of the work, and studies by Clark [BM 1933] and C. Brun [RV, X, 1919]. For an iconographic discussion we must mention Chastel [*Art et Humanisme à Florence . . .* 1959] who notes that, until then, the Nativity theme had been linked with the message brought by the angels and the joy it caused ; Leonardo, on the other hand, shows us a crowd in an uproar of surprise : around the central group, we do see a few celestial messengers represented as beautiful smiling creatures, but instead of celebrating in a lively manner this glorious event, they seem preoccupied, grave, as though the event was mysterious. In the background, the Magi's suite

the opposite side, give balance to that dramatic composition. Among the many sketches which are connected with this work — either hypothetically or definitely — two are of fundamental importance. No. 1978 in the Louvre gives us the first version of the 'story', an Adoration of the Shepherds in the courtyard of a palace in ruins, with two arcades on the left, flanked by two large staircases leading to a gallery, horsemen in the background, an ass and an ox, which disappeared completely from the final painting, the Virgin already in the centre, and a scattered group of worshippers. No. 436 in the Uffizi, in silver point on a pink ground, touched up with ink, bistre and white lead, with its derelict arches, its mysterious interrupted stairs and its pawing horses, is the immediate preparation for the background of the painting. Three sketches for a worshipping Virgin, seven for nude young men who might be shepherds, and other drawings in the Louvre, in the Musée Bonnat in Bayonne, in the Wallraf-Richartz Museum in Cologne, in the British Museum and in Windsor Castle, to which we add a most beautiful sketch in the Morgan Library in New York, have all been quoted by critics as possible preparatory drawings for that famous picture. Leonardo, says Chastel [*Art et Humanisme à Florence . . .* 1959], to intensify the psychological depth of the scene, freed the theme from the naive exoticism usually found in popular versions, and made it into an important episode of the history of humanity.

The picture is in an excellent state of preservation, but the

A drawing after 14 by Müller-Walde [1898], to show more clearly the sixty or so figures and horses which occur in the composition.

causes extreme excitement : they are fighting their way in complete confusion through people who have not yet understood what has happened ; two contrasting figures, a philosopher meditating on the left, and a young horseman, on

five panels on which it is painted have bulged slightly so that the joints between them show through the priming. It is more than a first draft : some parts show modelling and also colour, lacking only the very last touches. After the first sketch

A study of the perspective used in 14 (pen and wash, over traces of silverpoint, 163 × 290 mm.; Florence, Uffizi). (Below) early sketch for the same painting (pen and wash, 280 × 210 mm.; Paris, Louvre).

Leonardo drew over the priming the general design and all the outlines (see the roughed-out figures standing near the steps), leaving himself the possibility of adding or removing details; then he gradually darkened the figures leaving the background light; he filled the areas next to the floor with dark browns and then had to remodel the figures with black *impasto* to preserve the colour balance. In this way, he went over the whole of the first drawing and as the light background was swallowed up, touches of white lead replaced it as highlights. But this last more elaborate repainting remained half-done and the picture bears testimony of the various stages, from the standing figure on the right who only lacks the last colouring, to the figures on the left which show the various phases.

In spite of everything, this unfinished picture, born of a slow elaboration, has more spontaneity of expression than the preparatory drawings, in which the various motifs are isolated one after the other and sometimes studied in depth, whilst here they emerge, quivering with life, from the horses to the pressing crowd which forms a circle around the Virgin, dividing the pictorial space into a scene and a background, whose vanishing point lies on an axis just over the head of the Virgin. The hut which appeared in the preparatory sketch has disappeared and the dromedary has been replaced by a group of figures hardly indicated; behind two trees, a palm and an ilex, leading into depth, and at the foot of the two mysterious flights of stairs, an apparently disorderly medley and a feeling of fluid space. Nothing is left of the traditional Adoration and the kings and shepherds are replaced by a vast multitude of hands, of strongly characterised faces, of draperies fluttering out of the shadow of the human cluster on the one side and sucked on the other into a sort of luminous dust. They are neither magi nor shepherds, but living creatures with their faith and their doubts, with their passions and their sacrifices 'haloed' by the creative light of this masterpiece, in which colour would be superfluous.

15 ⊞ ⊗ 198 × 123 ▤ ⦂ 1483-86

The Virgin with the Young St John, the Infant Christ and an Angel (The Virgin of the Rocks) Paris, Louvre
For convenience sake, we shall also examine under this heading the cartoon with the same theme in the National Gallery in London (16).

This work is related to the theme of the dogma of the Immaculate Conception which was officially recognised by Sixtus IV in 1477. The original chapel of the Immaculate Conception in S. Francesco Grande in Milan, founded by Beatrice d'Este, wife of Galeazzo I before 1335, which originally sheltered Leonardo's painting, was destroyed in 1576 [Sant 'Ambrogio, AS 1908 (for the documentation only)] and the altarpiece commissioned by the members of the Confraternity was removed when the church was demolished. On 8 May 1479, the Brothers had assigned the painting of the vault of the chapel to Francesco Zavattari and Giorgio della Chiesa and in 1480, they asked Giacomo del Maino to provide a large, wooden altarpiece with carvings and reliefs, with empty spaces in the middle and on the sides intended for paintings, to be placed on the altar of the chapel, and they settled the amount due on 7 August 1482. Finally, on 25 April 1483, they made a contract with the painters Leonardo da Vinci and the brothers Evangelista and Ambrogio de Predis for the three panels, the gilding of the altarpiece and the colouring of the reliefs. From this fairly detailed contract, we learn the following facts : Leonardo – who was the only one to be given the title of Master – had no domicile of his own but was then the guest of the brothers De Predis in their residence at the Porta Ticinese (parish of S. Vincenzo in Prato) ; the three artists were bound to comply with their obligations and no distinction was made between them as to the distribution of the work ; the payment was to be 800 imperial *Lire* (200 ducats) apart from a larger sum which would be agreed on between Brother Agostino Ferrari and two brothers of the Confraternity to be chosen by the two sides, when the work was completed. A first payment of 100 *Lire* was to be made on 1 May 1483 and the remaining 700 *Lire* were to be paid in monthly instalments of 40 *Lire* from the following July to be completed between January and February 1485. The whole work should be completed by 8 December of that year (1483), the feast of the Immaculate Conception. As for the paintings, the central round-topped panel should contain a representation of the Virgin and Child surrounded by a group of angels and two prophets (probably Isaiah and David) and the two rectangular panels four singing angels on one side and four musician angels on the other. In the central compartment of the upper part, above Leonardo's painting, was to be a complicated relief dominated by God Almighty with the Virgin surrounded by angels, and beneath them a view of rocky mountains with the Crib, a first representation of the *Immaculata*. The contract stipulated exactly how it should be coloured. At the sides of the central relief, three

Other possible preparatory sketches for 14 (from the top); studies in profile: The Virgin nursing the Child, the Young St John, Nudes and Animals *(pen and wash [recto and verso of the same sheet], 405 × 290 mm.; Windsor, Royal Library);* Horseman fighting a Dragon *(pen, 138 × 190; London, British Museum);* Rearing Horse *(red chalk, 153 × 142; Windsor Royal Library), which has also been connected with 33.*

or four *capitoli*, that is rectangular fields with episodes from the life of the Virgin with small figures, cornices and frames, were to be gilded [ASL 1910.] So far, a detailed and even redundant contract, to which was added still a 'list of the ornaments' to make things even clearer for the artists. We suppose that Evangelista (who died about 1491) and his assistants were in charge of the frame (gilding, colouring and repainting), whilst Ambrogio painted the side panels with the angels, and Leonardo the central panel with the Virgin. We shall deal later with the striking differences between the iconography suggested in the contract and that actually used by the two painters. In a petition (published by Motta [ASL 1893] and assigned by him to 1493–4 after a paleographic examination), Ambrogio de Predis and Leonardo state that, having executed all the work mentioned in the contract of 25 April 1483, the centrepiece had required for expenses alone the 800 *Lire* agreed upon and duly paid ; they therefore asked for a further 300 ducats (1,200 *Lire*), in accordance with the conditions of their contract, but they were offered 'for Our Lady represented by the aforementioned Florentine' 25 ducats (100 *Lire*). Therefore, they asked the 'most illustrious and excellent prince' to intervene and either to persuade the commissioners to make an estimate and an offer under oath, or to appoint two experts, one for each party who could determine the value of the work, or to allow the two petitioners to withdraw 'the said Madonna, executed in oil', for which they had already received offers. Among the many hypotheses put forward in connection with this important document, nobody seems to have reflected on the fact that this appeal was obviously not the first, but rather the last move in a dispute which must have gone on for years. An appeal, beyond the ordinary judicial procedure, to the supreme ruler of the state (in this case Lodovico il Moro), is the last resort, the extra-judicial procedure which is attempted, when faced with a *fait accompli* above or after the process of law. This all goes to prove :
1) that the central part of the altarpiece was finished and had been handed over, without giving rise to any complaints about the work, since otherwise the appeal would be absurd and even more the suggestion, mentioned in that

93

15 Plates XXVII-XXXIV

16 Plates XXV-XXXVI

appeal, of a private sale of *The Virgin of the Rocks*;

2) that, after the delivery, the commission presided over by Brother Agostino Ferrari had met and been handed by the two artists the accounts for the 800 *Lire* they had received, and a request for an advance of a further 1,200 ;

3) that the commission offered 100 *Lire*. The two artists refused, and possibly appealed to an ordinary court of law. The Confraternity was a devotional association which did not have to account for its civilian or commercial transactions but only its eventual benefices, and so the first phase may well have been the order of 25 May 1486, through which the heads of the Concezione appointed four procurators *ad negotia*, that is for the litigation. But this suit could, in court of law, only go against the artists who had put themselves in the wrong by accepting in advance the judgment of the three commissioners. If the latter had settled for a supplement of 25 ducats, legally, the artists were bound to accept that decision : the appointment of those three could not result in a compromise or in a request for a technical report, and the threat to remove the central panel had no legal force. Therefore the appeal was necessary ; it had no result at first, but was again put forward by Ambrogio de Predis in 1503 and transmitted to Louis XII by the Governor of the Duchy. A rescript by Louis XII to the commander of Milan on 9 March 1503 mentions the appeal, signed by De Predis alone and therefore not the one quoted above, but substantially the same in context, asking him to take action after having heard the two sides. But on 23 June the Confraternity established, by

a notarial deed, Leonardo's absence from Milan and contested De Predis' request both for a valuation or the return of the painting. The case was therefore stopped a second time. The most important aspect of this document is that, in conjunction with the earlier ones, it makes it clear that the completed frame was delivered before the death of Evangelista and was put up in the chapel of the Confraternity. This document also confirms the dating of the work – now accepted by almost all critics – between 1483 and 1486. But in 1506 Leonardo, after seven restless years was on the point of returning to Milan, and De Predis, obviously armed with a power of attorney, re-opened the case and asked for the experts to be appointed : at the meeting of 4 April 1506 one of them was absent and an adjournment was obtained. On 27 April of that year an estimate of the work was finally made and recorded [Beltrami, RDA 1915 and 1918]. A new and unexpected circumstance emerged : the work was judged incomplete and Leonardo, who was still away from Milan, was requested *ad finiendum aut finiri faciendum* the painting within two years, and he was granted an account of 200 *Lire*. On 26 August 1507 and 23 October 1508 Ambrogio alone received the two payments and Leonardo, in a document of the same date, acknowledged them. That was the end of a dispute which had lasted twenty-five years and which, as far as we are concerned, has only one documentary sequel : the correspondence (mentioned by Carlo Decio and published by Verga [RV, II, 1906]) about the acquisition of the painting by the painter Gavin Hamilton

(from Count Cicogna administrator of Sta Catarina alla Ruota, which succeeded [1781] the Confraternity of the Immaculate Conception which had been dissolved), for 112 Roman *zecchini*, equivalent to 1582 Austrian *Lire*, in June-July 1785. The painting was then sold by the heirs of Hamilton to Lord Lansdowne, then to the Earl of Suffolk and was acquired by the National Gallery in 1880 for 9,000 guineas. At the time of the Hamilton sale, the picture was mentioned as being in a poor state of preservation and was doubtfully attributed to Leonardo, and by others to Luini. It is unquestionable, however, that the picture which is now in London, flanked by the two side panels by Ambrogio de Predis, which the National Gallery acquired later, is the same painting which, after the dissolution of the Confraternity, remained in S. Francesco Grande in Milan, and the one which was the bone of contention, if not from the beginning of the court case, at least when the two payments adding up to 200 *Lire* were made between 1507 and 1508. Leaving aside the question of possible collaborators, two points are now accepted by all scholars : the Paris version is earlier than the London one, the London version is not a copy but a deliberate variant with marked differences, not only because the slightly bigger figures, with simplified draperies, give a more monumental impression, but because the whole background

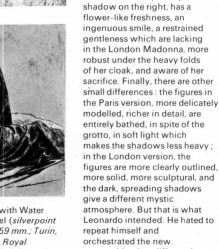

Studies connected with 15 (from the top, left); Rocks with Water Fowls *(pen; Windsor, Royal Library);* Head of the Angel *(silverpoint heightened with white, on yellowish ground, 181 × 159 mm.; Turin, Biblioteca Reale);* Plants *(red chalk and pen; Windsor, Royal Library);* Drapery of the Angel *(drawn with the brush, heightened with white on greenish ground, 215 × 160; ibid).*

is organized differently, with great attention to detail. Among the figures the angel must be compared first because of the famous pointing finger of the right hand which does not occur in the London version. But the drapery is also entirely different : in the Paris version it hides the anatomy of the figure whilst in the London one it

stresses it. In both versions the face is turned outwards but whilst in the Paris picture, with its slight smile and wide open eyes, it is turned towards the onlooker, in the London one it is more shaded and expresses inward meditation. The two figures of the Infant Christ seem identical but in fact they are different, not only because of the position, at a sharper angle to the spectator in Paris or because of the halo present only in the London picture : the kingly Jesus of the Louvre, unimpaired by the drastic restoration which has altered the transparency of the background and of the landscape, radiates a feeling of moral strength unequalled by the London Jesus, however beautiful. In London, the St John, through the heavier shadows, seems less lyrical although his facial expression appears to be same. The face of the Paris Madonna, without a halo, without any heavy shadow on the right, has a flower-like freshness, an ingenuous smile, a restrained gentleness which are lacking in the London Madonna, more robust under the heavy folds of her cloak, and aware of her sacrifice. Finally, there are other small differences : the figures in the Paris version, more delicately modelled, richer in detail, are entirely bathed, in spite of the grotto, in soft light which makes the shadows less heavy ; in the London version, the figures are more clearly outlined, more solid, more sculptural, and the dark, spreading shadows give a different mystic atmosphere. But that is what Leonardo intended. He hated to repeat himself and orchestrated the new composition in a different key. The darker colours, the blurred details, colours, transitions are not – or at least not always – the result of a less skilful hand, but the necessary accompaniment of an intentionally less luminous atmosphere. The fantastic cluster of rocks, which is reminiscent of the petrified reliefs of Mantegna, combines dreamlike magic and architectural precision and is almost identical in the two versions, except for the sky. But the aquatic vegetation is quite different and, in the Paris picture, reveals the evocative power of the artist.

If we want to reach an acceptable conclusion, we must first discard the hypothesis of a third version, begun in Florence, from which the two existing pictures would derive. That hypothesis was first put forward to confer authenticity on a beautiful altarpiece of the same theme in the parish church of Affori – smaller and only resembling Leonardo's picture in details. In any case, there is no trace among the drawings of any earlier design of such a new and striking composition, no record in contemporary documents and the problem is complicated enough without resorting to unsupported suppositions. Another hypothesis which we must also discard has been put forward by Reinach, Frizzoni, Malaguzzi-Valeri, and, more recently, by Davies and Clark and has been accepted by Nicco Fasola : according to that theory, Leonardo brought the first picture with him from Florence to Milan, and the London version was a copy of it. Against this one may argue – rightly in our opinion – that the atmosphere of the work, the *sfumato*, could only have been inspired by the landscape of Lombardy. But, there are two further irrefutable objections : the altarpiece, with its round top, and without any joints or reduction in size, fits perfectly within the frame designed by Del Maino and paid to him before Leonardo's arrival in Milan – a frame which could not possibly have been altered. And secondly the detailed contract of April 1483 would have been worded very differently if Leonardo had brought with him to Milan such an unusual and important masterpiece and if the purchasers had required a similar picture for their own altarpiece. And of course the Confraternity of the Immaculate Conception obviously had no idea of any difference of talent between the three painters. We suggest the following solution : at the time of the first appeal, soon after 1490, the picture inside the frame in S. Francesco Grande was the Paris version : *facta per dicto florentino*, that is, completed. For that picture, a collector had offered 100 ducats ; he might have been the King of France himself, acting through a representative ; and it is quite possible that already then the London version might have been sketched, with identical measurements, either for the unknown buyer or in the

Copies and derivations from 15 (from the top); copy in the church of Affori (Milan); copy in New York (?), Hurd Collection; copy in Benevento (?), Pedicini-Foglianise Collection; copy, attributed to De Predis, in Milan, Treccani Collection. (Below) a derivation, once attributed to Leonardo, in the Venice Seminary.

hope of making an exchange with the Confraternity. Or else, at the time of the second appeal (March 1503), the Paris version was still in the frame and the London one in the workshop of De Predis as a rough sketch since, to avoid an arbitration, the Confraternity of the Immaculate Conception quibbled about Leonardo's absence instead of using the more valid argument of the painting being in a very incomplete state. But the 1506 arbitration – whose text is missing – must have been concluded in the terms already stated at the time of the first appeal, that is decreeing that the 830 *Lire* received by the artists covered only the cost of the colouring and gilding of the frame, and perhaps the one of the two musician angels on the side panels which was painted by De Predis. At this point, it seems a logical deduction that the painting in dispute, which had not been paid even in part, should have been handed back to Leonardo who, out of gratitude or for reasons of profit, might have given it to the King of France, (who was compensated that way for the impossibility of taking away *The Last Supper*) for 100 ducats (400 *Lire*). In that way he also refused to be exploited by the rich members of the Confraternity who had refused for fifteen years to grant him his due. To them he gave the picture which was now well under way and which later became the London version. For this they paid, when it was finished, half of the sum they had been asked for the painting now in Paris. This is the only solution which accounts for the arrangements of 27 April 1506. It also explains Leonardo's insistence on recovering the painting and the unexpected reservations of the Confraternity about the painting being incomplete as well as the painter's willingness to finish the picture within two years. Therefore it is true, in a way, that both paintings came from S. Francesco Grande. The hypothesis of a substitution has already been put forward by A. Venturi and Poggi, who believed in a collaboration with De Predis, whilst Clark suggested Fernando de Llanos (see also Suida [1929]).

The London version, entirely designed by Leonardo in a sixteenth-century manner, with a change in some details and in the use of light, in the stronger modelling of the figures (recent cleaning has accentuated both its qualities and its blemishes), shows some collaboration – under control of the master – in the vegetation, the drapes, the faces and in some heavy shadows which are not entirely explained by the change of light and which Leonardo's general revision did not eliminate. The laboratory examination of both paintings, although helpful about their history, repainting and restorations, did not lead to any change of opinion [Hours, ADA 1953]. We must only mention that the transfer of the

Paris version onto canvas, at the beginning of the last century, was made by Fr Hacquin (1806), the great restorer who, in 1800–1 had transferred Raphael's *Madonna di Foligno*, a technical achievement which has remained famous.

There are many old copies, all of poor quality, of both the Louvre and the National Gallery versions, most of them by sixteenth-century Lombard painters. For example those in the Royal Collection in Copenhagen, in the Nantes Museum, in the Brera (by Bernadino di Conti) and in the Ambrosiana (by Vespino) in Milan, in the Victoria and Albert Museum (but for a time in the National Gallery) in London. Others, in private collections in Italy and in England are mentioned by Malaguzzi-Valeri [PA 1914, and *La Corte di Lodovico il Moro*, II, 1915]. The composition is also reproduced on an embroidery (of disputed date) in the Museo del Sacro Monte in Varese. Partial derivations are also numerous : one of them, with the figure of the Virgin and the rocks, was painted by De Conti (cf. the anthology on Leonardo da Vinci [1939, p. 50]) ; others use the figure of the Christ Child (in the Boltraffio altarpiece, formerly in Lodi, now in Budapest, and in a painting in the Seminario in Venice) or the young St John (in the picture by Cesare da Sesto in Elton Hall and in the *Pentecost* miniature by Antonio da Monza, in Vienna) or both *putti* (in a *tondo* published by Suida [1929]). The Perugino altarpiece in the museum in Nancy can also be considered as a derivation from *The Virgin of the Rocks*, at least as far as the Virgin and the two children are concerned ; and a curious mixture of elements from it also appear in a picture attributed to Sodoma which was in the Somzée Sale in Brussels (1904). For an original interpretation of the theme, Bernardino Luini deserves special mention : Suida [1929] was the first to attribute to him the beautiful copy in the Affori church, mentioned above. Other copies are probably by him too : in the Prado in Madrid, in the National Gallery in London (where the composition is reversed) and in a sketch in the Ambrosiana in Milan. Finally we can also trace the influence of *The Virgin of the Rocks* in a bas-relief in the Castello Sforzesco in Milan [Guida, 1957], from the early sixteenth century.

16 189,5 × 120 1503-06

The Virgin with the Young St John, the Infant Christ and an Angel (*The Virgin of the Rocks*)
London, National Gallery
This work forms a triptych with an *Angel playing the Vielle* and an *Angel playing the Lute* (on wood, respectively 117 × 60.5 cm and 118.5 × 60.5 cm) attributed to Ambrogio or to Evangelista de Predis. They

Derivations from 15 (from the top); painting attributed to B. de' Conti (Milan, Brera); others, by B. Luini (Madrid, Prado) and by an unknown artist (Paris [?], Thuélin Collection). The group of the two babies [below] in Naples [Capodimonte] is probably derived from a detail of the drawing (above) in Windsor (Royal Library).

were bought by the National Gallery in 1898 after belonging to the Melzi d'Eril Collection in Milan. The *Virgin* was bought by G. Hamilton in 1785 and immediately transferred to London. The following year, it was sold to Lord Lansdowne; then, after several changes of hands, it belonged to Lord Suffolk who was known to own it in 1824, and whose heir left it to the National Gallery in 1880. For other information, see 15.

17  27×21 *1490

Head of a young girl (*La Donna Scapigliata*)
Parma, Galleria Nazionale
A sketch in umber mixed with green through which can be seen either the white preparation or the roughness of a badly planed support, or the marks of the saw which was used to cut down the panel. In a fairly good state of preservation; attention has been drawn to small hollows from bore-holes and flaking off and various minute retouches – not old – done with less subtlety than the unfinished painting. These would seem to be ideal conditions for an undisputed attribution; but even in this case specialists do not agree. Most of them overlook this small picture, published by Quintavalle [E 1939] with ample historical documentation. It was part of the collection of Gaetano Callani, a talented painter and sculptor from Parma. Offered for sale by his son Francesco, it was bought, together with others, by the Parma museum in 1839 as 'a

18 42×33 *1490

Virgin giving the Breast to the Child (*Madonna Litta*)
Leningrad, Hermitage
This picture belonged to the Visconti in Milan and was inherited by the Litta, in the same city. Its traditional attribution was accepted when, in 1865, it was acquired by Tsar Alexander II for the Hermitage where it was immediately transferred from wood to canvas, with some noticeable damage. Vallardi [*Disegni di Leonardo da Vinci*, 1855] had published the drawing of the Virgin's head. This drawing was later acquired by the Louvre with the Vallardi Collection (No. 2376). The correspondence between the painting and the drawing, which Berenson dated from 1480–5 (*Disegni Fiorentini* [1961]), is so obvious that Berenson finally attributed the painting to Leonardo as unfinished, with a question mark. The battle of attributions started with Morelli [1880–6] who assigned the painting to

which Ippolito Calandra, in 1531, wanted to place in the bedroom of Margherita Paleologa, wife of Frederico Gonzaga, and perhaps the same which was listed in the Gonzaga inventory of 1627: 'a picture representing the head of a dishevelled woman, a rough sketch ... the work of Leonardo da Vinci' [Luzio, *Galleria dei Gonzaga*, 1913]. But Suida assigned it to Leonardo's school, and more recent critics do not take sides.

18

1902] and Wolynski [1907], whilst Harck [RK 1896], Seidlitz, A. Venturi, Hildebrandt and others chose the ubiquitous De Predis. For Bode, L. Venturi, Siren, Poggi and Bottari, the painting was the work of Milanese pupils on a design or cartoon by the master. We see again how difficult it is to define the personal characteristics of pupils, however talented. We must not forget, for what it is worth, the 'small picture slightly over one foot high, of Our Lady suckling the child, by the hand of Leonardo da Vinci, a work of great strength and beautiful finish', which M. A. Michiel saw in the house of the Contarini in Venice in 1543. The attribution to Leonardo was defended by Somof [Catalogue, 1899], Cook, [BM 1901] and Liphart [JPK 1912] (who noticed the influence of Bergognone on Leonardo). According to Goldscheider, the work was by Leonardo, but some details had been finished by Boltraffio. There is some similarity with the Munich *Madonna* (12) but the rhythm of the composition, the way in which the figure stands out against the background, the modelling, belong to a later period: not late enough perhaps to leave behind the Lombard character of the Leonardo school during the first stay of the master in Milan. There is a firmness of modelling peculiar to the quattrocento, the colours do not melt into *sfumato* in spite of the play of light and shade on the face. The drawings from the *Codex Arundel* (252 and 256, one pale blue sheet folded in the middle and dated March 1508, with the sketch of a head and two of children's feet) have not inspired this picture, but the Louvre head must have done so, although we might like to alter its 1490 dating. All considered, we believe that Goldscheider's hypothesis of a work by Leonardo completed by Boltraffio is the most

Bust of a Woman (*silverpoint heightened with white, on greenish ground, 180 × 165 mm.; Paris, Louvre*); *preparatory study for 18.*

Derivation from 18 (above); (Milan, Poldi Pezzoli) once attributed to Leonardo, now ascribed to one of his followers. (Below): (Milan, Borromeo Collection) attributed to B. de' Conti.

convincing. Brandi [FL 1967] also thought of Boltraffio, although he had doubts, but he excluded the possibility of Leonardo's hand, and believed that this rejection would pacify, at least temporarily, 'all' critics – which it did not. Horne's theory [1903] which connects this Virgin with an entry in Leonardo's notebooks in 1507–8 is without any foundation.

19 460×880 1495-97

The Last Supper
Milan, Convent of Sta Marie della Grazie (Refectory)
Two documents provide us with the date of execution, the date of completion and the exact theme of this picture. The first is a famous letter from Lodovico il Moro to the Marchesino Stampa, on 29 June 1497, saying, 'we particularly wish you to ask Leonardo, the Florentine, to complete the work he has begun in the Refectory of the Grazie, so that he can then attend to the other side of the refectory, and to obtain from him a signed agreement compelling him to finish it in a given time which he finds suitable' (Milan, *Archivio di Stato, Registro ducale*, s.n., c. 161). It is obvious that *The Last Supper* was at that time fairly advanced: we can assume that it had been transferred from the cartoons and was progressing quickly. Lodovico il Moro, who had already demolished the apse of the church, built by G. Solari, and asked Bramante to build, from 1492, the new apse and the cupola, had decided to enlarge and embellish the convent next to it. The new refectory must have been finished in 1495, when Donato da Montorfano painted a Crucifixion there. Chierici [PR 1950] has suggested that the idea of a new refectory and the commissioning of *The Last Supper* from Leonardo occurred to the duke at the same time; and his intelligent interpretation of the sources confirms this hypothesis, for we must remember that the commission to Montorfano was given, not by the duke, but by the Prior of the Convent.
The second document is Luca Paccioli's dedication to Lodovico il Moro of his treatise *De divina proportione* (8 February 1498). There he writes about *The Last Supper*: 'It is impossible to imagine the apostles more alive and attentive to the voice of ineffable truth and to the words: *Unus vestrum me traditurus est*. Each one of them seems to react with word and gesture, and our Leonardo has shown them worthily with his able hand' (Milan, Biblioteca Ambrosiana, MS 1499). It is impossible to deny that when that dedication was written *The Last Supper* was practically finished and even more to argue about the moment of the Supper depicted by Leonardo, since we know of the

17

small Leonardo da Vinci, a rare thing to find these days' and listed and illustrated as such in the catalogues of Martin [1872] and Pigorini [1887]. Ricci denied its authenticity and maintained it was a fairly late imitation, possibly by Callani himself. A. Venturi identified the small picture with the one

Bernardino de' Conti, possibly thinking of the variant by that painter in the Poldi Pezzoli Museum, which was also believed to be by Leonardo at a time when the Litta picture was accepted beyond doubt. This theory was accepted by Morelli, Berenson at first, Delarow [Hermitage Catalogue

The Last Supper *Plates XL-XLVI, with the lunettes above (20 A, B and C).*

friendship which existed between the mathematician and the painter.

We have another document for the year 1497, a passage from a lost account book of the convent, 'item for work done in the refectory where Leonardo painted the apostles, with a window : L37.16.5'.

There is no need to quote other documents nor to repeat descriptions of the work given in an exemplary fashion already by Goethe (we shall only list the characters, from left to right : Bartholomew, James the Less, Andrew, Judas, Peter, John, Christ, Thomas, James the Greater, Thaddaeus, Simon). But we must mention the few drawings connected with the painting. We must discard as a fake of later date the famous drawing (Venice Accademia, No. 254) — already condemned by Selvatico, Uzielli, Gronau, Hildebrandt, and four others even though Popham, Berenson [1961], A. Venturi and others believe it to be from Leonardo's school. This leaves us only No. 12542 in Windsor as a sketch for the whole. Although the subject is the same, this drawing is almost certainly earlier than the commission for the painting. Among drawings of draperies, arms and legs,

heads and caricatures which are numerous among Leonardo's manuscripts, some have been singled out as preparatory sketches for this or that detail. Discarding the beautiful heads in Weimar and Strasbourg (which are copies) we can only retain three from the Royal Library in Windsor as definitely connected with *The Last Supper*: the heads of Philip, Judas and James the Greater and a sketch of Peter's right arm (Nos 12551, 12547, 12552, 12546). The so-called Bartholomew and Matthew (Nos 12548, 12553) are doubtful. But the artist's meditations on the subject of *The Last Supper* find an echo not so much in his drawings as in one of his note-books : 'One of them, who was drinking, has left his glass in its place and turned his head towards the speaker. Another links his fingers tightly and turns with a frown to his companion ; another holds out his open palms, shrugs his shoulders up to his ears and gapes with astonishment. Another whispers to his neighbour and the latter turns towards him to lend an ear, holding a knife in one hand and in the other a half-cut loaf. Another, while turning round, knife in hand, upsets with his hand a glass over the table. Another lays his hands on the table and stares, another chokes over his mouthful of food, another leans forward to see the speaker' (London, Victoria and

Albert Museum, *Cod. Forster,* II, 2). We leave aside the anecdotes about the Prior and Judas' head, about the face of Christ which remained 'imperfect' because of the inability of the artist to render his ideal conception of it [Vasari] and the desire of the French King, Louis XII or François I, to have the wall cut away and to take the painting to Paris. This last story, given by Giovio and Vasari, is the only one which might contain a grain of truth.

The story of the painting through the centuries starts with Antonio de Beatis [*Relazione del viaggio . . . d'Aragona,* 1517–18], who found *The Last Supper* 'most excellent, although it is beginning to be spoilt, either by dampness oozing from the wall, or from some other negligence' [ed. Pastor, 1905]. Fifty years later, Vasari [1568] described the painting as 'so badly preserved that one can only see a muddle of blots'; Armenini [1587] pronounced it 'half destroyed but most beautiful'. *The Last Supper* was then ninety years old. Already three years earlier, Lomazzo [1584] had deprecated the use of oil instead of fresco, and particularly since the preparation was inadequate so that 'the painting is completely ruined' [1590]. Scannelli [1657] also quoted Armenini and described the state of the work : 'I went to Milan where I first of all went to see the so

Details of 19 (St Andrew [above] and [below] the table laid for the meal) during the last restoration. The control patches showing the state of the painting before restoration can be seen.

famous *Last Supper*, eager to discover its extraordinary beauty. I went at once to the refectory to fulfil my curiosity and I was most surprised and disconcerted to discover that only a few traces of the figures were left of this great work, and in such a blurred state that it was difficult to make out the well-known subject of the picture, whilst the heads, hands, feet and other naked parts of the bodies, painted in pale or medium shades were almost completely gone, and I expect that by now they have disappeared altogether. The figures all over the wall peeling off or otherwise damaged gave an idea of the remaining beauty of that work, which no longer has any effect, leaving the spectator to rely on its past reputation.' (the visit took place in 1642). The description is so detailed that various symptoms are singled out : condensation, rotting, mould, peeling off of the paint. After this account, there is no need to record the similar testimonies of numerous travellers and visiting artists such as Richardson [1720], or of Italian art lovers (Padre Monti and Gattico and Abate Gallarati).

A century and a half elapsed between the completion of *The Last Supper* and Scannelli's visit ; about the same length of time between Scannelli and the monograph by Domenico Pino [1796], and one hundred and seventy years between Pino and ourselves, but the ruin described by Scannelli still exists. Apart from its congenital technical defects, the passage of time, the assaults of the climate, the depredations of the French mercenaries in the sixteenth century and of Napoleon's soldiers in the eighteenth, it has withstood several more or less disastrous restorations. In fact, this long-suffering painting is a patient whose condition varies according to the weather, sometimes hiding itself in mist, sometimes allowing itself to be seen. An important document on the subject is a letter from Abate Gallarati to Vittorio Emmanuele, King of Sardinia : 'On days when the sirocco was blowing, a film of dampness spread over the painting, as if it had been exposed to the rain and it was impossible to distinguish clearly the outlines of the figures ; it was necessary to wipe it over lightly with a sponge or with a soft linen cloth. Therefore it is not advisable to cover *The Last Supper* with curtains ; if they are kept closed on rainy days, on the right side of Christ particularly, humidity gathers in such quantities that water can be seen trickling down the wall. And if the picture does not get air, it becomes covered with a fine white mould which would fade the colours more and more and spoil the painting. Restoration work started in 1726 : at that time, on the authority of Lomazzo and from its appearance, it was firmly believed that the wall was painted in oil. The first to put his hand to it was Michelangelo

Sketches connected with 19 (from the top); Head of Christ (painted over in tempera, 400 × 320 mm.; Milan, Brera), Study for St Philip (black chalk, 190 × 150; Windsor, Royal Library); St James (red chalk, 250 × 170; ibid.) ; St Peter (silverpoint on blue ground, 144 × 113; Vienna, Albertina); and for the same (black chalk, heightened with white, 165 × 155; Windsor, Royal Library).

Bellotti, who retouched the painting in general, patched it up and finally covered it all over with an oil varnish. As could be expected, this did more harm than good, and in 1770, Guiseppe Mazza began to scrape off Bellotti's repaints and was stopped in his work by the new Prior Paolo Galliani, a former pupil of the painter Lazzarini, who arrived just in time to save from destruction the figures of three apostles. Bellotti's restoration was condemned and praised in turn : condemned by C. Bianconi [1787] who also blamed the restorer for having started the custom of making a secret of his technique ; praised by S. Lattuada [1738], Ch. de Brosses [1738], Fr. Bartoli [1776], G. Bottari in his footnotes to the letters from Mariette to De Caylus [*Lettere*, 11, 1757]. We know that Bellotti's restoration had not destroyed Leonardo's painting through the very contradictions contained in Bianconi's accusations : he affirms that the original painting can still be seen in the three figures on the left which were not retouched by Mazza, but which had been treated by Bellotti. In 1802, the painter A. Appiani, entrusted with restoration work on the fresco, made a detailed study of its condition and concluded, like Padre Bosca [1672], that the main cause of the damage was a humid atmosphere, and that it was impossible to remove the painting from the wall. Then came S. Barezzi, who had successfully removed Luini's Pelluca frescoes. He stuck with strong glue the flaking off paint ; this work, which A. Venturi has described as 'disastrous', certainly did nothing to stop the deterioration of the painting. Efficient restoration started during this century with quite different methods, after the first chemical analyses of the plaster had been made by Kramer (1851) and Pavesi (1870). L. Beltrami, then Director of the Ufficio Regionale dei Monumenti in Lombardy, had the original windows re-opened in 1896, to create the same lighting conditions as when the picture was painted. A scientific committee of university professors (Carnelutti, Gabba, Murani) was asked to study the physical conditions of the atmosphere and the chemical components of the painting. Finally, after detailed close-up photographs (60 × 50 cm) of the heads and of the most damaged parts had been made, two preliminary studies were written. They were accepted (1904) and their author L. Cavenaghi, went on with the investigation by himself, and concluded it in 1908. From his report, excellent for that time, it was learnt that *The Last Supper* was painted in tempera over a complex preparation in two layers, the first rough-cast, the second mainly gesso, which was not damp proof. The numerous traces of previous restorations concerned mainly

Composition sketch for 19 (pen and ink, 260 × 210; Windsor, Royal Library).

Other preparatory sketches for 19 (from the left); Head of St Bartholomew (red chalk on red ground, 195 × 150; Windsor, Royal Library); Head of Judas (black chalk, with light retouches on red ground, 180 × 150; ibid.).

the draperies and the architecture, not the heads or faces of the figures, except for Philip and the top of the table. Before starting on the cleaning, Cavenaghi consolidated the surface of the painting with 'gum dissolved in suitable solvents which were as little influenced as possible by the changes in moisture'. But all this work and all those precautions were not enough since O. Silvestri had to attempt another rescue operation in 1924 with gum dissolved in petrol, and again in 1930 there was talk of mould and of the corrosion of organic substances used by previous restorers, and a new cleaning was necessary. It was later undertaken by M. Pellicioli, who first had to rebuild the refectory, partly destroyed by an air raid in 1943. With modern technical methods of restoration at his disposal, he first consolidated the picture and then carefully removed the repaints – some of them centuries old – which covered parts of the original painting. A considerable part of the table top, of the heads of Bartholomew and Philip, of the body of Judas and of the hands of Christ emerged, and the whole painting became much lighter in colour.

There are innumerable copies of *The Last Supper* (see C. Horst [RV 1930-4]), some of them made during Leonardo's life-time. We must mention, as a proof of the great fame of the painting, one attributed to Solario, formerly in the convent of the Hieronymites in

Castellazzo (fresco) ; those by M. A. Anselmi, painted about 1530 in the church of S. Pietro Martire in Parma, now destroyed, and by A. Araldi in the convent of S. Paolo, in the same town, from about 1514. Others : one in the Royal Academy in London, previously in the Certosa of Pavia attributed to Giampetrino, which is very faithful to the original ; one in the Louvre, attributed to Marco d'Oggiono ; one in the Hermitage ; a fresco by B. Luini in Sta Maria degli Angeli in Lugano ; one in the parish church of Ponte Capriasca, remarkable on account of the addition of two scenes, *The Agony in the Garden*, and *The Sacrifice of Isaac* ; and one in the chapel of Revello (Saluzzo) ; in the Vercelli Museum, from a local convent of the Humiliati, in the archbishop's palace in Milan ; in the church of the Assumption in Morbegno ; in St-Germain-l'Auxerrois in Paris ; in the Museum of Teramo (Abruzzi). In the Brera (Milan), there is a beautiful drawing by Gaudenzio Ferrari. Cardinal Borromeo commissioned from Vespino (1612–16) a faithful copy of the painting, which is now in the Ambrosiana in Milan. Bossi's copy, which was destroyed by the 1943 bombing, was famous and the one in Castelgandolfo is similar. In 1816 G. Rafaelli, under Bossi's direction, made a large mosaic copy for the Austrian government which had it placed in the church of the Franciscans in Vienna.

Coats of Arms surrounded by Garlands of Foliage Milan, Convent of Sta Maria della Grazie (Refectory)

They consist of linked coats of arms from the houses of Sforza and Este. The garlands are made of various plants. They occupy the three lunettes over *The Last Supper* (19) and are therefore unanimously attributed to Leonardo. They were ruined by cleaning, probably in the eighteenth century and some attempt was made to improve their condition when *The Last Supper* was restored in 1854. Very little of the original painting is left. (For further details, see 20 A, B and C.)

20 ⊞ ⊗ base 225* 1495-97 ▤ ⦂

A. In the left lunette, at the sides of the shield, the following inscription, in a very bad state of preservation : *MA [ria] M[a]X[imilianus] SF[ortia] AN[glus] CO[mes] P[a]P[iae]*, referring to Massimiliano Sforza, son of Lodovico il Moro, to his title of Count of Angera, and to his lands near Lake Maggiore and in Pavia.

20 ⊞ ⊗ base 335* 1495-97 ▤ ⦂

B. The inscription in the central lunette : (*LV[dovicus] MA[ria] BE[atrix] EST[ensis] SF[ortia] AN[glus] DVX[Mediolani]*) refers to Lodovico il Moro and his wife Beatrice d'Este and to their ruling over Angera and Milan.

21

20 ⊞ ⊗ base 225* 1495-97 ▤ ⦂

C. In the right lunette, one can make out : *SF[ortia] AN[glus] DVX BARI* which refers, apart from Angera, to the Duchy of Bari, to which Lodovico had been appointed by Ferrante of Aragon.

21 ⊞ ⊗ —— ▤ ⦂

Portraits of the Dukes of Milan and their Sons Milan, Convent of Sta Maria delle Grazie (Refectory)

The figures, which time has worn away to shadows, are inserted in pairs (base about 90 cm each) in the signed (and dated 1495) *Crucifixion* by Giovanni Donato di Montorfano (on the wall facing *The Last Supper* (19), as worshippers : on the left, Lodovico il Moro with his eldest son Massimiliano ; on the other side, the duchess Beatrice d'Este with her son Francesco. Their attribution is a typical example of the sort of mistake which can be caused by tradition. Vasari wrote in 1568 : 'While he was working on the Last Supper, in the same refectory on the end wall where there is a painting of the Passion in the old manner, he portrayed Lodovico himself, with his eldest son Massimiliano and on the other side the Duchess Beatrice with his other son Francesco, both of whom later became Dukes of Milan, all of them beautifully painted.' And Lomazzo [1584] : 'In the Refectory of the Convent delle Grazie can still be seen, by the hand of Vinci, the portraits of Lodovico and Beatrice, both kneeling, with their sons in front' ; and Padre Gattico in his description of the convent (Milan, *Archivio di Stato*) : 'Leonardo painted . . . the duke and the duchess whom we see by the side of the said Jerusalem, and those portraits have decayed because they were painted in oils, against the painter's will, but on the order of Duke Lodovico'.

Faced with such overwhelming documentation, some critics had doubts, but nobody dared deny that those coloured blots on the Montorfano fresco had originally been painted by Leonardo, in spite of their later decay and superimposed repaints. As a result of the 1943 bombing of the refectory, the few traces of original colour were taken away, so were the restorations and the plaster surface, and remains of the design in red ochre appeared, revealing without doubt that Leonardo could never have been their author. Obviously Vasari's great authority misled Lomazzo, who was already blind when he dictated his *Trattato*, and all others after him. And what about Lodovico's letter ? It probably meant that the duke intended to have the whole wall painted.

22 ⊞ ⊗ —— ▤ ⦂

The Redeemer Formerly in Milan, Convent of Sta Maria delle Grazie

In the *Catalogus Superiorum Cenobii Ord. Praed. S. Mariae Gratiarum*, compiled by Padre V. M. Monti (Milan, *Archivio di Stato*), two other paintings by Leonardo are listed : one is 23 (see below) and the other was in the lunette over the door between the convent and the church, with the figure of Christ as Redeemer which, probably in a bad state of preservation, was destroyed in 1603 when the doorway was widened.

23 ⊞ ⊗ —— ▤ ⦂

Our Lady of the Assumption with St Dominic and Peter of Verona, Lodovico il Moro and Beatrice d'Este

Formerly in Milan, Church of Sta Maria delle Grazie

Listed by Padre Monti together with the preceding work (see 22), this picture was also in a lunette, over the main entrance to the church next to the convent. In 1594 it was almost completely ruined and was replaced by a painting by Graziano Cossali, more or less a copy, which was re-copied again by Bellotti when he restored *The Last Supper* [Malaguzzi-Valeri, 1915]. Cossali's receipt stated : '1594, 13 October ; given to Master Gratio for the execution of the painting placed over the church door, 20 ducatoni'. His picture bears no trace of Leonardo's inspiration but does not *a priori* disprove the entry of Padre Monti, who was a most conscientious and reliable compiler. It is confirmed by the story of the convent by Gattico [Amoretti, 1804 ; Pica and Portaluppi, *Le Grazie*, 1938].

24 ⊞ ⊗ 1498 ▤ ⦂

Interlacing Branches Milan, Castello Sforzesco (*Sala delle Asse*)

The name of Leonardo is mentioned in connection with work planned for the Castello Sforzesco, in two letters from Gualtiero da Bascapè to Lodovico il Moro, dated 20 and 21 April 1498 and published by Calvi [*Notizie*, 111, 1869]. They are the only irrefutable documents about this work, which must have been lengthy and complicated for various reasons. In the first letter, we read : '. . . for the *Saletta Negra*, Messer Ambrosio [the duke's engineer, Ambrogio Ferrari] has come to an agreement with Master Leonardo, so that he

(*Above and below*) *two partial views of the decoration of the* Sala delle Asse *in the Castello Sforzesco in Milan* (24) *in its present state: an angle of the vault with tree trunks rising from the walls; and the central part, with the family arms of Duke Lodovico il Moro.*

Some of the many known copies of 19 (above, from the top); the Ponte Capriasca version (Lugano) attributed to Francesco Melzi; the Louvre version, ascribed to Marco da Oggiono. (Below) the famous copy engraved (1800) by Raffaello Morghen after a drawing by Teodoro Matteini.

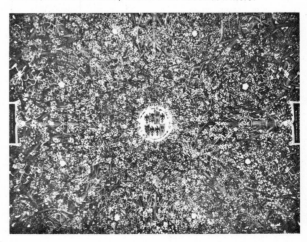

should lose no time in completing the work', and in the second: 'On Monday, the centering will be removed from the large *Sala delle Asse*, that is the one in the tower. Master Leonardo has promised to complete the decoration during September'. In the *Saletta Negra*, which has been located by L. Beltrami, no traces of any work by Leonardo was found. But in the *Sala delle Asse*, on the ground floor of the large square North tower, fragmentary and damaged remains of a large decoration were revealed when the whitewash was removed from the ceiling in 1893. They allow us to reconstruct the decorative scheme, which consisted in a vault covered with foliage entwined round trellis-work, with tree trunks corresponding to the corbels of the sixteen lunettes and dividing at the corners into leafy branches interlacing with golden cord and forming bowers and involved designs at regular intervals; imposing shields on the corbels between the lunettes interrupted the trellis work which in the centre was finished off with a cord twisted into geometrical figures around the duke's armorial bearings. Beltrami published a drawing survey of the original remains [E 1919], but there is no photograph before E. Rusca's repainting in 1901–2, done very accurately, but too heavily. During the 1956 restoration, Ottemi della Rotta uncovered a lunette and a small part of the vault, painted in tempera and in a very bad state, and proved that Rusca had tried to follow as well as he could the fading outline. Ottemi della Rotta also found traces of an old restoration, probably dating from the sixteenth century. Recently, a small stretch of monochrome painting in Leonardo's manner was discovered behind the benches: it consists of clusters of rocks rising from the floor, twisted roots, small plants and a tree trunk rising towards a corbel of the vault. The hypothesis that this large decorative scheme was executed by Bramante [Malaguzzi-Valeri], has now been discarded almost completely. The sophisticated geometrical phantasies on the vault must be at best a stiff academic copy of the original. Even the original was not by Leonardo's hand, but rather by assistants working on his designs. It is known that for the decoration of the *camerini*, left unfinished in 1496, Leonardo had much help: '. . . two masters continually drawing on my pay and expenses . . .'. Obviously we cannot imagine Leonardo reproducing over the vault identical decorative elements. For that reason, many Leonardo scholars, such as Goldscheider [1952] have removed this work from the master's catalogue. But it was certainly his idea to translate into wall paintings the ephemeral foliage decorations which were used for public festive occasions at that time. This vault, which was completed in five months, between May and October 1498, strikes us as the most original abstract design of the time, based on geometrical forms clothed in foliage – not really classical since it tends to fill all available space, not really Gothic because of its rhythm. Between 1400 and 1500, it was a unique achievement.

Detail of the original design of 24 from a copy made by L. Beltrami [1902].

25 43×31 *1490

Portrait of a Musician
(Franchino Gaffurio [?]) Milan, Pinacoteca Ambrosiana

The Musician is the first of a series of controversial portraits from the Milanese period. After the visit of Antonello to Milan (or at least his stay in neighbouring Venice) about 1475, the tradition of portrait painting became famous throughout the valley of the Po, and Leonardo was generous with his ideas and his teaching and put at the disposal of everybody in his workshop his large repertory of designs: 'his assistants paint portraits and he puts his hand to them all in turn' [Pietro da Novarella, 1501]. If we consider his habit of working on and off with long interruptions on the same picture, and his way of always intervening in the most difficult part of the works painted by his pupils, we are not surprised that the most learned and discerning specialists cannot come to an agreement about attributions. This work is typical of such difficulties. It is not listed in the bequest of Cardinal Borromeo to the Milan Accademia, which formed the nucleus of the Ambrosiana (1618), in which appears the *Dama delle Perle* (26) as 'Portrait of the Duchess of Milan, work of Leonardo da Vinci'. Therefore this small picture was not part of this famous group of works. However, we find it, with the lower part already repainted, in the 1686 catalogue, as a 'half-length portrait of a Duke of Milan with a red cap, by the hand of B. Luini'; with the attribution later corrected to 'by the hand of Leonardo'. The 1798 inventory describes it as 'school of Luini'. But in the second part of the nineteenth century, comparisons of technique, measurements and type with the above mentioned female portrait caused both pictures to be attributed to Leonardo as likenesses of Lodovico il Moro and Beatrice d'Este. When the identification was proved to be impossible, in the case of the male portrait, because of discrepancies with the appearance of the duke, other noble names were mentioned, with arguments based on conflicting historical reports and documents. All these useless flights of erudition were swept away when, in the course of a reorganization of the Ambrosiana Collection in 1904, the picture was examined closely. Obvious repainting was removed from the lower part, as

25 Plate LXII

traces of previous brushwork or at least preparation could be seen through it. The operation, directed by Cavenaghi, led to the discovery, under the black and yellow clothes, of the sitter's right hand holding a scroll, on which could be seen the lines and notes of a musical score and, partly erased, the letters '*Cant . . . Ang . . .*' [Beltrami, RV, II, 1906]. The musician was identified, with some reservations [Id.], as Franchino Gaffurio, the choir-master of Milan Cathedral, who frequented the duke's court and was certainly on friendly terms with Leonardo. He was born in 1451 and therefore would have been the right age to fit in with the portrait painted between *The Virgin of the Rocks* and *The Last Supper* (15 and 19). Gaffurio is the author of a *Practica Musica* printed in 1496, which includes woodcuts designed by Leonardo, according to Gerolamo D'Adda, and of *Angelicum ac divinum opus* (only printed in 1508) to which the words on the inscription could refer: '*Cant-um Ang-elicum*'. Although this identification seems to us the most likely, various other musicians whose presence in Milan or in other courts at that time is known, have been suggested in turn. For instance the famous Jean Cordier from Bruges, who was eminent at Lodovico's court until 1496; Angelo Testagrossa (*Cant-or Ang-elus*), who was the singing master of Isabella d'Este; and Atalante Migliorotti, the musician who came to Milan with Leonardo – a hypothesis based on a note by Leonardo himself ('a head of Atalante looking up') which suggests the possibility of a portrait. Beltrami put forward another hypothesis, which has never been investigated, according to which the painting came from the collection of Gaspare Molla, a Roman die-caster who left in his will (1630) all his pictures to the hospital of S. Carlo al Corso, including 'the head by B. Luini, with a black frame' (similar to the frame which surrounded *The Musician* for centuries), which could have been transferred to Milan because of the connections between the Ambrosiana and the Roman church dedicated to a Milanese saint.

If it is authentic, this painting is the only known male portrait by Leonardo; it is unfinished and in a perfect state of preservation: the face and hair in the foreground are entirely finished; the clothes, the hand and the scroll are an advanced sketch. But is it really by Leonardo's hand? Non-specialist readers will again be amazed to learn that so many distinguished critics, from Morelli onwards, have been unable to isolate any typical elements sufficient to recognize Leonardo's portrait manner, although we do have one portrait universally acknowledged to be entirely by his hand: *The Mona Lisa* (31). Scholars who accepted the painting as authentic were, after Beltrami, Cook, Ricci, Schiaparelli, Bode, Liphart, Suida, Berenson (after 1935) and more recently Goldscheider, Clark and Heydenreich. Ambrogio de Predis is suggested by Morelli, Seidlitz, Frizzoni, Carotti, A. Venturi, Malaguzzi-Valeri, Poggi, Hildebrandt. Cagnola and Castelfranco are undecided. Bottari does not accept the attribution to Leonardo. Sirén ascribes it to Boltraffio. The main stylistic arguments put forward to support the attribution to Leonardo are the expression of the eyes which is similar to that of the angel in the Louvre *Virgin of the Rocks*, and the strong light, reminiscent of Antonello, which models the face in the same way as in his anatomical drawings.

26 51×34 *1490

Female Portrait (*The Lady with the Pearl Hair-net*; *Beatrice d'Este* [?]) Milan, Pinacoteca Ambrosiana

Because of locality, size and other traditional reasons already recorded (25), this profile portrait was at one time linked with that of *The Musician*. It was illustrated in *Musaeum* and listed in the collection of Frederico Borromeo, given to the Ambrosiana (1618), as a 'half-length portrait of a Duchess of Milan, by the hand of Leonardo', and as such was taken to Paris in 1796. On its return to Milan, it was considered as a portrait of Beatrice d'Este. But when it was discovered that the so-called duke was in fact a musician and not part of the Borromeo gift but had probably come from Rome, the traditional story collapsed and the two pictures were considered separately. Morelli, identifying the profile with the portrait seen by Michiel in 1525 in the house of the Contarini family in Venice, attributed it to De Predis and believed the sitter to have been Bianca Maria Sforza. Various hypotheses were then put forward about the identity of the sitter, none of them based on any definite documents: for Mündler, she was Isabella of Aragon, the wife of Gian Galeazzo Sforza; for Carotti, a lady from the Trotti family; for Motta, Domitilla Trivulzio; for Schiaparelli, Anna Maria Sforza. Beltrami gave up the idea of Beatrice and thought of Cecilia Gallerani. And there were others. But we consider that a definite identification of the model would only be of interest if it could help us to identify the author of the portrait; we shall therefore not enter into those detailed controversies based on research into history and costume and shall only discuss the attribution. Müntz, Beltrami, Bode, Liphart, Mather, Gronau, Müller-Walde and Schiaparelli attributed the portrait to Leonardo. The last named assigned to Leonardo all the female portraits under discussion and to strengthen his theory and to include the portraits in the Montorfano *Crucifixion* (21), which was then believed to be by Leonardo, he maintained that Leonardo, during that period, either deliberately or to suit the taste of his patrons, adopted the local Lombard portrait tradition and imitated the technique of Antonello. This theory would be acceptable were it not dealing with Leonardo, who was indeed influenced by Lombardy, but by the atmosphere, the light and shade, the wide horizons and not by the local technique or iconographic tradition. Mori attributed the portrait to De Predis and was followed by Frizzoni, McCurdy, Seidlitz, Schubring, Bodmer, Berenson, Poggi, Malaguzzi-Valeri, Sirén and Hildebrandt. Some critics did not take sides: Séailles, De Bourdelles, Evelyn, and, more recently, Goldscheider. Suida ascribed it to De Predis, with interventions by Leonardo. A. Venturi, De Rinaldis, and possibly Castelfranco, believe the painting might be by one of those unknown painters who imitated Leonardo. Recently,

26 Plate LXIII

Longhi suggested [1940 and 1956] an attribution to Lorenzo Costa about 1492.

27 ⊞ ⊘ 54×39 *1485-90 ▤ ⋮

Portrait of a Lady with an Ermine (*Lady with a Ferret* [*with a Marten*]) Cracow, Czartoryski Museum
Prince Adam Czartoryski acquired this picture at the end of the eighteenth century and gave it to his wife for her private collection in Pulany Castle. In the manuscript catalogue of the collection there is no mention of the place or date of the acquisition but, from other indications, it was probably in France during the revolution. The spurious inscription 'La belle Feronière – Leonardo d'Awinci' was probably added at the castle. Its previous history is completely unknown, it is certainly a work from Lombardy, and from Leonardo's school (1483–90). We believe that the animal represented is an ermine – not because the sitter might be the fascinating Cecilia Gallerani, but because the little creature is white and the symbol of chastity, whilst the marten,

27 Plates XXXVII-XXXVIII

28 Plate LXI

apart from its colour, was associated with lasciviousness. No lady, however broad-minded, and particularly no princess, would have accepted to be represented with a marten and no painter would have dreamt of suggesting it. The state of preservation, fair at first sight, is in fact rather poor, the background has been redone, the outline has been retouched and the left side of the figure has been corrected. Only the face is intact, except for a pink glaze, and the ermine.

The picture was brought to the attention of the critics by Müller-Walde who published it [1889] as a work by Leonardo,

whilst Rosenberg [1898] considered it as a variant or copy of the so-called *Belle Ferronnière* in the Louvre (28) and Müntz described it as a poor painting, unworthy of the master and even of his school. From that time, the attribution was disputed between Leonardo, De Predis and Boltraffio. Antoniewicz ascribed it again to Leonardo [1900] and suggested the name of Cecilia Gallerani for the sitter. He was followed by Bode, Suida, Carotti, Schaffer and, after the painting had been examined in Dresden by Voigtlaender, Möller, Bock, Beltrami, Hildebrandt, Clark, Goldscheider and, in the 1936 lists, by Berenson who had previously attributed it to Boltraffio, as did A. Venturi. Other scholars who attributed it to Boltraffio were Loogan, Pauli, Sirén, Gronau and Poggi. Malaguzzi-Valeri, Hewett, and Seidlitz agreed on the name of De Predis. Therefore, in spite of the state of preservation of the painting which makes stylistic examination less reliable, the majority of critics attribute it to Leonardo, and Goldscheider even describes it as the most fascinating portrait painted by the master. One of the arguments in favour of this attribution is the possibility of identifying the work with a portrait not mentioned by historians, but well documented by contemporary writers, which Leonardo painted of Cecilia Gallerani. This portrait, celebrated by the court poet Bernadino Bellincioni who died in 1492, was sent by the sitter to Isabella d'Este in 1498, to allow the duchess to compare Leonardo with Giovanni Bellini, warning her at the same time that 'she had been portrayed as immature and her appearance had since altered completely'. Dates correspond with the probable time of the painting. Cecilia Gallerani and Leonardo were certainly on friendly terms, moreover the face in the picture is very similar to that of the angel in the first version of *The Virgin of the Rocks* and even more to the preparatory sketch (Turin, Biblioteca Reale, No. 15572). Cecilia was born about 1465. Her father was Fazio, a Milanese nobleman who was ambassador to Florence between 1467 and 1470, an important land-owner in the district between Carrugate and Brugherio and the son of the General Treasurer of the Duchy. Cecilia was seventeen and an orphan when Lodovico gave her the domain of Saronno. During ten years she reigned over his court through her beauty, her intelligence and her gifts of integrity (she always remained faithful to the cause of the Sforza, and had to flee into exile for their sake). After Lodovico's marriage, she became the wife of Count Bergamini di Cremona and lived in the Palazzo Broletto (formerly Carmagnola) in Milan. If the Cracow portrait is really hers, there should be no

X-ray of the central part of 28. Technical discrepancies with The Mona Lisa (*31*) *are difficult to appraise because of the different woods (oak for the former, poplar for the latter). The hair did not originally hide the ear and only did so after a restoration which also affected the part to the right of the face.*

doubt about Leonardo's authorship. There is a subtle correspondence, both iconographic and psychological, between the eager look of the lady and that of the little animal and a symbolic correspondence between the names : Gallerani and γαλῆ in Greek, meaning a weasel. Like the juniper of Ginevra Benci (7) and the knots (*vinci*) in the decoration of the *Sala delle Asse* (24), a pun on Leonardo's own name. Recent photographic, X-ray and chemical examinations [Kwiatkowski, 1955] have revealed that the paint is extremely thin, smooth and even, without any trace of brushwork except on the hair and on the ermine, and in the latter there might even be brushwork done with the left hand. But none of this will convince disagreeing specialists. Whether she was Cecilia or not, we believe that the lady with the ermine is by Leonardo's hand, possibly with assistants working on the corrected or repainted parts and that the composition is akin to that of *The Musician* (25).

28 ⊞ ⊘ 62×44 *1490-95 ▤ ⋮

Female Portrait (*La Belle Ferronnière*) Paris, Louvre
The first reference to this picture as a work by Leonardo and the portrait of a Duchess of Mantua can be found in a passage by Pierre Dan [*Trésor des merveilles de Fontainebleau*, 1642]. It must have been part of the king's collection since the days of Louis XII or François I. It is obviously a Lombard portrait from the circle of Leonardo, and is

beautifully painted. The date, according to the critics, varies between 1482 and 1497. It was confused with a portrait of the 'Belle Ferronnière', who was a mistress of François I, by Bailly in his inventory of the king's pictures in 1709 (Louvre, No. 1605). The two pictures, both attributed to Leonardo in Lepicié's catalogue (1752–5) exchanged names, all the more easily that 'Ferronnière', which was the name of François' friend, also happened to mean, in the sixteenth century, the ribbon which ladies tied round their forehead to hold their hair in place. As for the so-called *Belle Ferronnière*, its traditional attribution to Leonardo remained unchallenged until 1894, when Frizzoni, the most brilliant of Morelli's disciples, removed the painting from the already dwindling list of authentic works to place it within the wider labelling of 'fifteenth-century Milanese school' [ZBK 1894]. Berenson agreed at first, but later assigned the picture to Boltraffio, then again to Leonardo. From then on, there were two opposing camps. The attribution to Leonardo was accepted by Rosenberg, Müntz, Solmi, Taylor, Jacobsen, A. Venturi and Schiaparelli. Boltraffio's supporters were Löser, McCurdy, Carotti, Bodmer, Pauli, Seidlitz, Malaguzzi-Valeri, Sirén, Ochenkowski. Suida and Goldscheider thought it was predominantly by Leonardo, but finished by Boltraffio. Clark stressed the powerful face, and the intense eyes which suggested the hand of the master. Frizzoni was in favour of a more general

attribution to the school or workshop and was followed by Poggi, Hildebrandt, De Rinaldis, Bottari. Finally, Singer (C 1915], supported by Rosenberg, suggested, because of facial similarities, that *The Ferronnière* and *The Lady with the Ermine* (27) are portraits of the same person and by the same hand, whether the hand was Leonardo's or not.

As we can see, the age-old attribution to Leonardo, endorsed till 1839 by the great critical authority of Waagen, was mainly supported after 1894 by critics from the old school, whilst the younger generation was in favour of Boltraffio's authorship. But nowadays there is a cautious return to the old theories, backed by recent scientific examinations in the laboratory of the Louvre, which have revealed a technique similar to that of *The Mona Lisa*, if we take into account the difference between a painting on oak instead of poplar wood and the many restorations and repaintings which have altered the arrangement of the hair, originally pushed back over the ears [Hours, ADA 1953]. If the hypothesis of Singer and Rosenberg, which on grounds of similarity, is acceptable, were confirmed by some documents, this magnificent creature could well be (and we say 'could' because even in the case of *The Lady with the Ermine* we are not sure of the identity of the sitter) Cecilia Gallerani, and in that case the picture would have been painted between seven or ten years later than the Cracow portrait. If we admit this hypothesis, and if we accept that the same artist painted both, it seems impossible, if this artist was Leonardo, that Cecilia should not have mentioned it to Isabella d'Este when she sent her the portrait which she found 'so imperfect a likeness'. There is however an undoubted similarity between the two ladies, one still young and thin, the other more mature. But in that case, the present portrait would have been painted between 1492 and 1495 and Leonardo's portrait manner would show little progress. That is why we discard the vague suggestions about a portrait of Elisabetta Gonzaga [Müntz (attributing it to Leonardo)] of Beatrice d'Este [Helvet (attributing it to De Predis)] or of some other lady, and still doubt that the sitter could be Lucrezia Crivelli [Gault de Saint-Germain, 1803; Amoretti, 1804] if the painter was Leonardo. Three learned Latin epigrams [*C. Atl.* 167 v.] show without any doubt that Lucrezia was the mistress of Lodovico il Moro and that Leonardo painted her portrait ; and according to contemporary documents, Lodovico, about six months after Beatrice's death, gave Lucrezia Crivelli various lands near Lake Maggiore and Lake Como and granted her the right to leave them to her son Gian Paolo born in 1497. It was probably during those years that Leonardo was asked to paint her. But if the Louvre portrait is by Leonardo, it would have been painted about ten years later than *The Lady with the Ermine* and only eight years before *The Mona Lisa*. X-ray comparisons in the Louvre laboratory with Boltraffio's *Madonna Casio* show a great difference in the technique and seem to exclude the possibility of its being painted by Leonardo's closest disciple, but planned and revised in draft by the master himself.

29  63×46 *1500
Portrait of Isabella d'Este
Paris, Louvre
Black chalk and pastel with touches of red on the hair and flesh, and of yellow on the dress; in a poor state of preservation. It is pricked for transfer and the perforation is inked over the forehead and nose. Probably after the transfer, Leonardo finished the

29 Plate XXXIX

(*Above*) copy of 29, possibly by A. de Predis, formerly attributed to Leonardo, (*Florence, Uffizi*). (*Below*) drawing (*silverpoint on pink ground, 320 × 200 mm.; Windsor, Royal Library*) sometimes connected with 29.

30 Plates L-LIV

sketch as an independent work of art [Berenson]. It was in the Calderara-Pino, then Vallardi Collection [*Disegni di Leonardo . . .*, 1855] and was acquired by the Louvre in 1860 for 4,410 francs, as the portrait of an unknown woman. There is a replica, or early copy in the Uffizi, by De Predis, according to Goldscheider. Another one in Oxford, formerly in the Leighton Collection in London [cf. *Vasari-Society*, II]. According to Goldscheider [1952], only the head is by Leonardo; the dress, the bust and the hand are by a bad pupil who also touched up the profile. Seidlitz [1909] attributes it to Boltraffio. Gruyer dated the sketch about 1500 and Ch. Yriarte [GBA 1888], starting from that date, identifies the picture with one of the two documented portraits of Isabella executed by Leonardo. This hypothesis — based on comparisons with the medal by Giulio Romano, and another anonymous one — was accepted by Rosenberg and Müntz. Luzio and Malaguzzi-Valeri disagreed. But most art historians since then have followed it and it now seems fairly certain.

Leonardo is known to have painted two portraits: one is mentioned by Lorenzo Gusnasco who, when he sent a Spanish lute to Isabella (13 March 1500), wrote: 'Leonardo Vinci is in Venice and has shown me a portrait of Your Highness which is a very good likeness. It is beautifully painted, it could not be better' (Mantua, *Archivio di Stato*). The other portrait, which remained in Mantua, is mentioned by the Marchesa herself in a letter of 27 March 1501 to Pietro da Novellara: Ask him [Leonardo] to send another sketch of our portrait because our noble husband has given away the one which he left here . . .' (*ibid.*) It is fairly likely that Leonardo, who never complied with Isabella's

(*Above*) two studies for 30. Black chalk (*160 × 120 mm.; Paris, Louvre*). Another (*160 × 145 mm.; Windsor, Royal Library*) sometimes related to 35. (*Below*) drawing (*Vienna, Schlumberger Collection [?]*) believed autograph, but a copy of 30.

repeated requests for a painting by his hand, might have done the present third sketch from the portrait in his possession. Without getting involved in the detailed controversies to which this work gives rise, let us note that the Louvre drawing, if we take into account the quick sketching of the bust and right hand, is all by one artist, and with conception and execution so close to each other that Berenson is certainly right when he maintains that it was done in one sitting.

30  159×101 *1498*
St Anne, The Virgin, the Infant Christ and the Young St John
London, National Gallery
Black chalk, heightened with white; together with 29, it is the only cartoon which has survived of the many which Leonardo must have drawn for his important works. We shall ignore all the phantasies woven around the theme of the composition and shall only record the oldest interpretation; that of the agent of Isabella d'Este who saw the attitudes of the characters, as symbolic of the negative attitude of the Church towards the Virgin's efforts to hinder Christ's Passion. There are many known preparatory sketches and drawings: firstly the British Museum drawing (No. 1875.6.12.17; from the Galichon Collection) which shows the Virgin and St Anne inscribed in a rectangle. Another related small study, in simple pencil outline, together with a male head (also in the British Museum) was published by De Rinaldis (Plate 66). The well-known sketch R.F. 460 in the Louvre is, in the design of the two women, closer to the cartoon than to the Louvre painting (35). Berenson also mentions Nos 12533 and 12534 in Windsor Castle: the first in black chalk, the second in black and red chalk with touches of ink and heightened with white, which are studies for the heads of St Anne and of the Virgin. The first one is obviously connected with the picture even though the saint looks younger; the second is less evident.

A letter of Padre Resta to Bellori throws some light on the history of the famous cartoon: 'Before 1500, Louis XII commissioned a cartoon of St Anne from Leonardo da Vinci, who lived in Milan: Leonardo made a first sketch which is now in the house of the Counts Arconati in Milan'. Resta was wrong to connect the 'sketch' with an unlikely commission by Louis XII since it would have been difficult for the king to have contacts with an artist who then belonged to the Sforza court and who, on his side, had so little respect for the new lord of the duchy that he sent his money to Florence and went off to Mantua and Venice. But Resta knew the second, different, cartoon of which he believed he owned the original and his record is valuable. The other 'sketch' is none other

than the London cartoon which, from the Arconati went to the Casnedi in 1721, and from them to the Sagredo in Venice. There, it was acquired in 1763 by Robert Udny, the brother of the English Ambassador in Venice and in 1791 it was already mentioned in an inventory of the Royal Academy, from which the National Gallery bought it in 1966.

The cartoon represents a closely-knit monumental group; the Virgin turns round with a display of draperies which reminded Berenson of the Parthenon goddesses by Phidias; and the heads of the two women are close together. It was certainly drawn in Milan before 1500, but not necessarily for the French. Hildebrandt and Seidlitz date it from the early Milanese period between 1483 and 1494; Clark, about 1498. This last dating, later than *The Last Supper* (19) seems the most acceptable. It is unlikely that the cartoon was ever used for a painting by Leonardo or

(*From the top*) derivations from 30, by B. Luini: Holy Family with St Anne and St John the Baptist (*Milan, Ambrosiana*) *and* Virgin with the Butterfly (*Budapest, Szépmüvészeti Muzeum*). (*Below*) derivation from 30 (*Milan, Borromeo Collection*), attributed to Boltraffio.

his pupils since we have no record or copy of such work. But the subject was taken up by Bernardino Luini, with the addition of a St Joseph, in a painting in the Pinacoteca Ambrosiana. The cartoon, which inspired various isolated figures by Melzi, Solario and Sodoma, was in fact in Luini's possession and was inherited by his son Aurelio, according to Lomazzo.

31 77×53 *1503-05

Female Portrait (*Gioconda*; *Mona Lisa*) Paris, Louvre
We owe the two most usual names of the picture, *Gioconda* and *Mona Lisa* (the latter is mainly used in Anglo-Saxon countries) to Pozzo and Vasari.

This is the only portrait by Leonardo whose authorship has never been seriously doubted in the course of four centuries and a half. The only others which are also universally accepted are his Turin *Self-portrait* in red chalk (p. 84) and the cartoon with the profile of Isabella d'Este (29), although the latter has been questioned by one or two critics. *The Mona Lisa* is backed by documents, although they do not agree in every detail. It is first mentioned in the diary of Antonio de Beatis; after a visit to Leonardo at Cloux, on 10 October 1517 he noted 'three pictures, one of a certain Florentine lady painted on the request of the late Giuliano de' Medici, another of the young St John the Baptist, and one of the Virgin and the Infant Christ sitting on the lap of St Anne, all most perfect'. And Vasari wrote [1550 and 1568]: 'For Francesco del Giocondo, Leonardo undertook to execute the portrait of his wife, Mona Lisa. He worked on this painting for four years and left it still unfinished; and today it is in the possession of King François of France, at Fontainebleau.' The detailed description which follows does not refer to the composition or landscape, but only to the face. In fact, his description was probably written from hearsay (since Vasari had not seen the painting) or from a copy, unless he used an earlier description. But this cannot have been his main source, the Anonimo Gaddiano who only noted: 'He made a portrait from nature of Pietro Francesco del Giocondo'. This could either be a *lapsus calami*, or a reference to a portrait unknown to us. The third testimony is that of Cassiano del Pozzo, who saw the work in Fontainebleau in 1625: 'A life-size portrait, on wood, framed in carved walnut wood, representing the bust and head of a certain Gioconda. This is the most complete work from that artist, and she only lacks speech'; a description follows, in which the landscape is not mentioned, the portrait is compared to Greek statues, the bad varnish which has been added is deplored and the attempts of the Duke of Buckingham to obtain the picture, which was considered the most beautiful of that time,

31

are retold. In 1642, Father Dan [*Trésor*], stated that the work had been acquired by François I for 12,000 francs (4,000 gold *écus*). The picture is again mentioned by Peirez [1625 MS, Paris, Bibliothèque Nationale], Le Brun [Catalogue of the collection of Louis XIV, 1683], Paillet [Versailles Catalogue, 1695], Bailly [Catalogue of the Cabinet of Paintings in the Tuileries, 1706 and Versailles Catalogue, 1709]. In 1760 it was in the room of the director of the Royal Palaces [Seurat Catalogue], in 1800 Bonaparte had it taken back to the Tuileries and in 1805 he placed it in the Salon Carré of the Louvre. There, it was stolen on 21 August 1911 by a certain Vincenzo Perugia, who was working in the museum as a house-painter. He took it to Italy and tried to sell it to Alfredo Geri, a Florentine art dealer, who immediately informed the Soprintendenza. On 21 December the painting was returned to France, but it was first exhibited in Italy, one day in the Uffizi in Florence, one day in the Galleria Borghese in Rome, and two days in the Pinacoteca di Brera in Milan.

Leonardo must have started the portrait about 1503. The age of Lisa Gherardini, born in 1479, who married in 1495 Francesco Bartolomeo del Giocondo, would fit that date. But are we sure that she was the sitter? We are told by Vasari that Mona Lisa sat for the portrait and again by Cassiano del Pozzo who however read Vasari's *Lives* and repeated the statements of the greatest and at that time almost the only writer on Italian art. But Antonio de Beatis, visiting Leonardo with one of the most famous cardinals, learnt in front of the picture, and obviously from Leonardo himself, that it represented 'a certain Florentine lady painted from nature on the request of the late Giuliano de Medici'. And consequently a friend of the latter, whose portrait we are told, he gave back to Leonardo when he married Philiberta of Savoy. All this is possible; it is possible that the friend of 'the late Giuliano' was Giocondo's wife and it is also possible that the painting which De Beatis saw was another portrait and not *The Mona Lisa* which, in October 1517, already belonged to the king. But it is not possible that the portrait could have been painted in Rome about 1513, as has been suggested, since the drawing Raphael made from it cannot be later than his stay in Florence in 1505–6. It is very strange that no single document, no record of payment, no vague mention in Leonardo's notebooks or in contemporary letters should have survived about this picture which is considered as the highest achievement of portrait painting of all times. Not even sketches by the artist, unless we count the hands in the cartoon of Isabella d'Este or a drawing at Windsor (No. 12558), which Müntz alone connects with *The Mona Lisa* but which probably dates from the time of *The Virgin of the Rocks* (15). If any real place has inspired this dream landscape, which is both unreal and as accurate as a panoramic view, with its different planes, its damp atmosphere and its melting snow, this place will not be found on the banks of the Arno, but rather in Lombardy with its autumnal mists. There might even be a resemblance with Leonardo's well-known sketches of the countryside near Lake Lecco. To return to the painting: it was probably cut at the sides where two columns of about seven

Probably a preparatory drawing for 31 (silverpoint, heightened with white, on yellowish ground, 210 × 145 mm.; Windsor, Royal Library). It is sometimes connected with 7 A.

X-ray of the central part of 31, showing its perfect state of preservation. The vertical stripes are caused by the different thicknesses of the poplar wood.

centimetres are faintly visible; it is still on the original poplar wood and seems absolutely intact, without a single repainting throughout the centuries (no other painting on wood can boast such an exceptional *craquelure*). Nobody has dared remove the layer of varnish which protects it better than glass, but at the same time darkens and tones down the colours. (Only recently, after X-ray and technical examinations was the surface smoothed in places where infinitesimal differences of level occurred

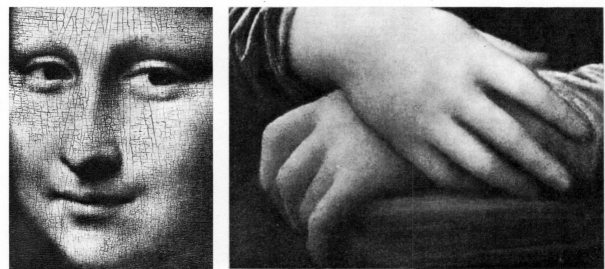

Details of 31 examined in raking light and showing through the difference of the craquelures *that different media were probably used for face and hands, which would account for the variation in colour between them.*

   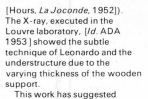

The X-ray, executed in the Louvre laboratory, [*Id.* ADA 1953] showed the subtle technique of Leonardo and the understructure due to the varying thickness of the wooden support.

This work has suggested idle and elaborate comparisons with archaic Greek sculpture, with the enigmatic smile of the *Korai* and of the Etruscan Apollo, with representations of the meditating Buddha, with Agnolo Firenzuola's suggestions about different kinds of smile, classified in his small treatise on beauty [*Perfetta Belleza*, 1541]. Recently more refined theories have been put forward, more in keeping with the latest iconological tendencies: let us mention at least the 'cosmological' interpretation [Ivanov, RE 1952] according to which the portrait incarnates the *anima mundi* as Marsilio Ficino understood it. In fact, this picture is not merely a portrait. It constituted the painted autobiography of the artist and reflects his unique personality, his intellectual affinities, his knowledge, his genius and his unattainable ideals. These ideas are translated into the instinctive grace of a human, but exceptional face. What matters here is not only the monumental aspect of the picture, obtained through a miraculously subtle modelling which suggested to Sir Kenneth Clark the likely hypothesis that Leonardo started from a nude study in his preparatory cartoon (which also explains the many nude *Mona Lisas* of French imitators); what matters is not only the plastic synthesis of an infinite number of minute observations or the simultaneous existence of different planes of vision which seem to tend towards a total perception: what matters most is the revealing coexistence of a natural creation and of the human vision of that creation expressed lyrically and movingly.

There are many copies and imitations (some of them notorious through claims that they are the 'true' original, or an autograph replica), variants and derivations. Some of the earliest are in the Prado in Madrid, in the museums of Munich, Baltimore, Tours and Bourg-en-Bresse. A survey organised in Paris in 1952 discovered at least seventy-two old copies. Many of them are in private collections, two of which deserve to be mentioned: one in the Lee Collection in Fareham and one belonging to an English collector [cf. De Hevesy, GBA 1952; Isnard, JA 1957; Pulitzer, *Where is the Mona Lisa?*, 1966]. Variants on the nude Mona Lisa can be found in the Hermitage (believed by Waagen to be by Leonardo's own hand, but in fact an old copy from the Chantilly cartoon), in Hampton Court (attributed to Bernardino Luini), in the Musée Condé in Chantilly (cartoon by Joos van Cleeve), etc.

(*Above, and right*) *some of the most characteristic copies of* The Mona Lisa (*31*): *one published* (*1967*) *by H. Pulitzer* (*London*) *as by the hand of Leonardo, and those in Rome* (*Parliament*), *Innsbruck* (*Luchner Collection; possibly by Salaino*), *Tours* (*Musée*); *Madrid* (*Prado*); *and Tours* (*ibid.; with a lace bodice*).
(*Below*) *some free interpretations: Raphael, drawing for his* Maddalena Doni *in the Pitti* (*Paris, Louvre*); *School of Luini,* Mary Magdalen (*formerly in Montreux, Cuenod Collection*); *Joos van Cleeve,* Young Woman (*formerly in a German collection*); *wax bust* (*Berlin, Staatliche Museen; previously attributed to Verrocchio, then to Leonardo, but in fact a nineteenth-century fake*). (*Second row down*) *derivations from a supposed study by Leonardo of the nude model: cartoon in Chantilly* (*Musée Condé; previously attributed to Leonardo*); *and paintings in Palanza* (*Kaupe Collection*), *Leningrad* (*Hermitage; once attributed to Leonardo*), *Bergamo* (*Accademia Carrara*). (*Bottom row*) *variations on the* Nude Mona Lisa *in Dijon* (*Musée*), *Washington* (*National Gallery*); Diane de Poitiers, (*signed by Clouet*) *and previously in Paris* (*Collection de Janzé; Gabrielle d'Estrées and the Duchess of Villars*).

  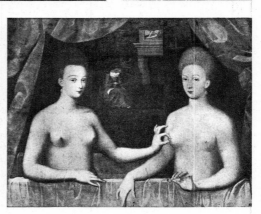

Pride and fall of the Mona Lisa

Apart from her influence as a prototype of beauty, The Mona Lisa has a history of her own, unlike that of any other work of art. The persistence of nude representations (p. 104), supposedly based on a lost study by Leonardo, was already a sign of morbid curiosity for an extraordinarily famous work. The growing obsession with the picture only developed about the middle of the nineteenth century, after the interpretations of the aesthetes: The Mona Lisa became the most famous painting in the world and her image began to be used freely in various ways. The average thickness of her paint was calculated (3,68 mm.), the relation between her height and her breadth (1.45283 . . .), the volume of the imaginary cylinder whose circumference would be the width of the picture (17,209.13 cm³), and so forth; out of her 4,081 cm² it was also calculated that 199.2 were occupied by the face, 166.89 by the right hand, 826.94 by the landscape, etc. The measurements of the sitter were 'reconstructed' (height, 1.68 m. or 1.73) and her vital statistics. Her pose was said to be that of a pregnant woman; her celebrated smile must have been due to asthma; finally, even her sex was doubted: Isarlo claimed [Combat, 1952] that 'she' was a young transvestite (fig. XXXIV). The 1911 theft enhanced her fame even more and inspired novelists, song-writers and humourists. A postcard was published (III) with the caption: Je vais retrouver mon Vinci; others celebrated her homecoming (VI); a whole 'commemorative' series represented actresses dressed as The Mona Lisa, from the Belle Otéro (XXXII) to Mistinguett, and the exploitation of this gold mine included even Fernandel (XXXIII). Soon, the theme was also used for political propaganda, producing (1918) a postcard with the Kaiser-Mona Lisa (VII), followed more recently by many others such as the Stalin-Mona Lisa (VIII). Meanwhile, she has become a household word (for instance, in French, the phrase: Connu comme la Joconde) and in Paris there are innumerable bars, bistros, and restaurants called: A la Joconde. She has also been used to advertise cheese, oranges, gramophone needles, cigars and ladies' shoes in Italy, Spain, Holland and England. Her name is an unfailing password everywhere. The German post office has used the painting on a stamp (XXXI). At the same time she has given rise to many iconoclastic manifestations on postcards (I, II) or cartoons (even in Russia [IV]), but they were friendly jokes and could also be taken for tokens of admiration. With Marcel Duchamp however, in 1919 (IX), attacks on The Mona Lisa took on the meaning of a protest, of the rejection of a commonplace ideal which was above all a symbol of academic museum culture, of 'beauty'; many others endorsed that protest, from the then revolutionary Dali (X) to Gruel and Suyeux (with a short film [XIII, XVI]), from J. Harold (XI) to M. Henry (XIV) and Souzouki (XV). The protest became, with the followers of Pop-Art – anticipated by Fernand Léger (XII) – an irony all the stronger that the breaking up of the picture was done purely through photography (which, with the Englishman L. Vala, revealed The Mona Lisa's profile [XXX]), as if to suggest that the defects they magnified were already within the painting. At the end of 1965, the gallery of M. Fels in Paris organized an exhibition of those phantasies on The Mona Lisa, by painters of all nationalities (XVIII, XIX, XXII); but none of them equalled the invention of the German photographer A. Felling (XXIX) and of the Frenchman J. Margat who in a special edition of Bizarre (1959; with a cover by Siné [XVII]) went from a harmless translation into a photographic negative (XXI) to an optical deformation (XXIII), to a letter-press adaptation (XXIV), and from dissociations and reassociations of the elements (XX, XXV-XXVII), through irreverent deformations (XXXV, XXXVI) to reach final destruction (XXXVII).

I-VIII

IX-XV

XVI-XXII

XXIII-XXX

(XXI-XXXVII

32 ⊞ ⊗ ── ≡ ⦂
Virgin and Child (*Virgin with the Yarn Winder*)

Pietro da Novellara, writing to Isabella d'Este on 4 April 1501 mentioned 'a small picture which he painted for a certain Robertet, a favourite of the King of France [Florimond Robertet, the Secretary of State for Louis XII] . . . a Virgin sitting as if she meant to wind a spindle, whilst the Child, his foot over a small basket, has picked up the yarn winder and is gazing at the four arms which make up the shape of a cross, smiling eagerly at the cross and holding it fast, refusing to give it back to His mother who is trying to take it away from Him'. This is a concrete and irrefutable testimony, but no trace of any sketch of that sort has survived among Leonardo's papers. There are three variants on this theme, which must have been inspired by the missing cartoon or by sketches of the master: *The Madonna* in the Reford Collection in Montreal, which was attributed to Sodoma, one belonging to

Putative originals of the lost painting 32, in (from the top): Drumlanrig Castle (Scotland), Duke of Buccleuch; Montreal (?). R. W. Reford Collection; Munich, collection of Prince Rupert.

Prince Rupert of Bavaria and a third from a private English collection, which entered art history with the famous exhibition at the Burlington Club in London in 1898. From those variants and from the inspiration they gave to Raphael and Francabigio, Suida [*Studi in onore del Verga*, 1931] suggested 1506 as the date of Leonardo's painting, which, he thinks, was completed in Milan by a pupil. But for this date, Suida does not take into account the document of 1501, which cannot be doubted; and for the place Milan is more likely than Florence, to judge from the origin of the variants we know. Suida also points out that none of the three variants corresponds exactly to Pietro da Novellara's description: the position of the Virgin is probably, and that of the Child certainly, different, and there is no basket. We suspect that Leonardo's imitators, whether they be called Sodoma or by another name, dropped the symbolism of the cross-shaped yarn-winder and concentrated on showing Jesus consciously yearning for the instrument of his future Passion: the shortening of the horizontal part of the cross and the absence of the spindle basket seem to justify such a hypothesis.

33 ⊞ ⊗ 1504-06 ≡ ⦂

The Battle of Anghiari

The work originated in August 1504 with a commission by the Gonfaloniere P. Soderini for the decoration of the *Sala del Gran Consiglio* or *Salone dei Cinquecento* in the Palazzo Vecchio in Florence, asking Leonardo to represent the Battle of Anghiari, and Michelangelo the Battle of Cascina (see *The Complete Paintings of Michelangelo* (9). The theme assigned to Leonardo referred to the battle of 29 June 1440 in which the Florentine

(Above) famous copy by P. P. Rubens (Paris, Louvre) from the central group of 33. A more faithful and older copy (below) by an unknown artist, in Florence (Uffizi). (Centre) another sixteenth-century copy of 33, possibly from Tuscany (Naples, Doria d'Angri Collection).

Recto and verso of a sheet (192 × 188; Budapest, Szépmüvészeti Muzeum) with preparatory studies for 33.

(Below, from the left) preparatory studies for 33: Encounters of Horsemen (pen and wash, 147 × 155 mm.; Venice, Accademia); Skirmishes between Horsemen and Infantrymen (pen, 165 × 153;).

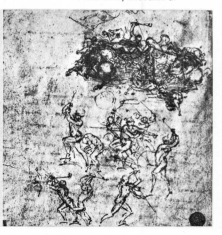

army, allied to the Pope's army under the command of Orsini, defeated — near Anghiari in the region of Arezzo — the army of the Duke of Milan, led by Piccinino. Vasari has described in detail the central episode of Leonardo's painting.

But by an irony of fate, apart from this detailed account, this work, of which nothing is left, is the best documented of all Leonardo's paintings. There are no less than twenty records including the long account in the *Codex Atlanticus* (74 r.) not in Leonardo's hand, which was probably written by Machiavelli; also the allocation (24 October 1503) of the *Sala del Papa* and neighbouring rooms in Sta Maria Novella in Florence, to allow Leonardo to design the cartoon; also the draft of an agreement signed on 4 May 1504, with details of obligations, remuneration and time limits; also various payments and expenses during that year, in connection with the execution of the cartoon; until February 1505, by which date the cartoon should have been finished. And in 1505, from 28 February, we have payments for the building in Florence by Giovanni di

Andrea, the father of Benvenuto Cellini, of an articulated scaffolding in the *Sala del Gran Consiglio* in the Palazzo Vecchio. And again, payments for Leonardo's assistants, and for his expenses such as plaster, linseed oil, pitch, white lead etc to prepare the wall and begin the painting. We learn from all those documents that a ream and 29 quires of sheets of paper were used for the cartoon, 88 pounds of flour to paste it together, and 3 sheets of cloth to line it. To prepare the wall, 673 pounds of plaster were needed, 89 pounds of pitch, 223 pounds of linseed oil, 48 pounds of white lead and 36 pounds of whitewash. With those ingredients, Leonardo tried to make up the stucco preparation which he had read of in Pliny [Anonimo Gaddiano] and which would allow him to proceed slowly and methodically in the execution of his grandiose work. He tried the preparation successfully on a wooden panel, and managed to dry it with heat. But in the large room he failed miserably.: the fire which he lit was not sufficient and the preparation became runny. However something remained of the battle of horsemen around the standard, which he painted on the wall, since they are mentioned by Albertini [*Memoriale*, 1510]; since in 1513 the painted wall was repaired; and since Doni, advising Lollio in 1549 about the things which were worth seeing in Florence, told him to walk up to the 'large room and look at a group of horses and men . . . a fragment of a battle by Leonardo da Vinci which you will find miraculously beautiful'. But when the room was transformed into the *Salone del Cinquecento* Vasari painted his frescoes on the wall in 1557. As for the cartoon, the central part, translated into painting, was probably in the *Sala del Consiglio*, the other part in Sta Maria Novella in the *Sala del Papa*, in 1505 or at the beginning of 1506 when Leonardo interrupted his work. A recently discovered autograph note in the *Madrid Codex* (II, 2 r.) says: 'On Friday 6 June 1505, as the thirteenth hour was ringing, I began to put the colour in, at the palace. As I was lifting my brush to begin, the weather got worse and I had to call back my assistants because the cartoon tore, the water container was upset and suddenly it started raining violently and it became as dark as night'.

There are few copies of the work and only of the central encounter. Apart from a poor contemporary print, the most faithful copy is in the Reserve of the Uffizi and seems to have been designed from the painting itself since its unfinished appearance might correspond to the spoiling of the original. Another copy, mentioned and reproduced by Poggi, belongs to the Horne Museum in Florence. But the

Derivations from the lost Leda. *(From the left) the ex-Spiridon version (132 × 78 cm.; on wood) in Rome. The painting (112 × 86) in the Galleria Borghese in Rome, formerly attributed to Leonardo. (Below) a later copy (Paris, Louvre) once believed to be the original, probably the most faithful of all.*

(Below) studies for the lost Leda: *drawing (pen over black chalk, 200 × 160 mm.; Windsor, Royal Library); another sketch (pen heightened with white, 175 × 145; ibid.)*

most famous and the most lively is a composition by Rubens (Paris, Louvre) — naturally, a copy of a copy. Nothing remains of the cartoon, neither a sketch of the whole, nor definite references to the episodes at the sides, except perhaps a sheet by a pupil of Raphael's, in Dresden. The sketches by Leonardo's hand which could refer to this work consist of a pencil drawing of two heads belonging to figures in the central group and the profile of a warrior with the helmet missing (Budapest, National Museum); a battle of horsemen and (at the bottom of the sheet) of infantrymen; another battle of horsemen with a horse carrying a standard; another still in which the horses themselves fight ferociously (Venice, Accademia); a galloping horseman; horsemen and warriors; heads of savage-looking horses and the head of a man screaming (Windsor Castle). Neither Vasari's description, nor the copies, nor the drawing of Rubens 'full of satanic fury' will ever make up for the lost painting: all we have is secondary testimonies and, we believe, the central fragment of a fight of which we know nothing.

34 ▦ ◑ *1510-15 ▤ ⦙

Leda
The earliest evidence concerning this painting is provided by the Anonimo Gaddiano: '. . . and [he] also [painted] a Leda'; but those words were later crossed out, which may be why Vasari does not record the painting. But Lomazzo mentions it three times: in *Idea* [1590]: '. . . the finished works (although they are few) of Leonardo da Vinci, like the nude Leda and the portrait of the Neapolitan [sic.] lady Mona Lisa, which are in France'; in the *Trattato* [1584] where, talking about downcast

eyes as a sign of modesty, he adds: 'Leonardo da Vinci applied this when he represented Leda completely nude, with the swan in her arms, and casting down her eyes in shame'; and also in a sonnet of his *Grotteschi* [1587]. Lomazzo never went to Fontainebleau where Cassiano del Pozzo saw the picture in 1623, and described it in detail: 'A Leda standing, almost completely nude, with at her feet the swan and two eggs, from which four babies have come out (Castor and Pollux, Helen and Clytemnestra). It is somewhat dry in style, but exquisitely finished, particularly the woman's breast. The landscape and foliage are represented with great diligence. But it is in a bad state since it is made up of three panels which have split apart and the painted surface has been broken'. It appears again in an inventory of 1692–4 [Müntz]: 'A Leda painted on wood by Leonardo da Vinci'. Eighty years later, in 1775, Carlo Goldoni wrote to Venanzio de Pagave: 'There is no memory of its existence [the *Leda*'s] in France. I have seen paintings and examined various old royal registers and catalogues and also the list of the pictures which have been destroyed. Not only is De Vinci's Leda not there, but French professors and amateurs pretend that she

never was there and that he never painted such a picture.' Perhaps the original work, which was already in a bad state of preservation in 1623 had been lost without leaving a trace. The documentation about the painting is completed by a reference to a cartoon by the master in 1721 in the house of the Casnedi in Milan: 'A Leda standing, nude, with Cupids in one of the bottom corners', recorded by Wright [1730]. The existence of a cartoon for *Leda* is confirmed by Raphael's pen drawing, executed about 1505, during his stay in Florence (Windsor, No. 12759), which is very close to the version of the painting in the Galleria Borghese in Rome, including the unmistakable arrangement of the hair (this motif inspired one of Raphael's philosophers of *The School of Athens* in the Vatican *Stanze*). Direct evidence about *Leda* however is rather poor and consists of a sketch on sheet No. 156 r. of the *Codex Atlanticus* (mentioned by Müller-Walde [JPK 1897]), of a drawing in Weimar and of

(Above) a derivation: the Half-kneeling Leda (34) probably by Giampetrino (Neuwied, Prince of Wied). (Below, and bottom row, from the left) drawings connected with 34 in: Windsor (Royal Library; detail), Rotterdam (Boymans Museum; detail 126 × 109), and Chatsworth (Duke of Devonshire; pen, 155 × 140).

107

35 Plates LV-LIX

·137·

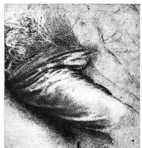

studies for the hair in 12515 and 12516 in Windsor, in which the expression and the attitude of the woman's head represented are directly linked with *Leda*. Thiis [1914] also connected with the painting a beautiful drawing with a rainy landscape, No. 12409 in Windsor. A. Venturi suggests that the Parma drawing (17) could be connected with *Leda*, and also a sketch in the Ambrosiana, which Berenson does not mention. We conclude that Leonardo certainly designed *Leda* during his second stay in Florence, and may have finished the painting during his second stay in Milan. The first hypothesis rests on the existence of Raphael's drawing, the second on the fact that most surviving copies, contemporary or workshop, were made by artists from Lombardy. Of the nine variants catalogued by De Rinaldis, two deserve our attention because they are by far the best. The first is the ex-Spiridon version, which Berenson finally believed to be by Leonardo's hand, or at least done in direct collaboration [1916] and which was shown, in a somewhat dilapidated and dirty state in the 1874 Paris exhibition for the benefit of Alsace and Lorraine. It then belonged to the Marquis de la Rozière who left it to his heir the Baron de Roublé, whose widow in turn sold it to Ludovic Spiridon who, for three years, had it carefully cleaned and restored. Spiridon's heirs sold it to the German minister H. Goering, and after the war the picture was returned to Italy where it became the property of the State. The precise, marble-like, almost neo-classical style does not suggest the hand of Leonardo; the landscape of water, foliage and houses is too stilted and polished for him. However we are not convinced by Hoogewerff's theory [CO 1954] according to which the figures are by Melzi and the landscape by Joos van Cleeve. The second variant, in the Borghese Galleria, is in a good state of preservation and of unknown origin, and is listed as Leonardo's work in the 1693 inventory, which attribution was handed down until Piancastelli [1893]. It differs from the ex-Spiridon version in many points, mainly the landscape, the hair arrangement, the babies (only two: Castor and Pollux) who are much bigger in relation to their mother, the egg which is whole and partly hidden, the swan's wing which clings to the woman's side down to the knee, like an elegant curve; little shrubs and small Flemish-looking animals and birds make the landscape quite alien to the master's style. Everything leads us to believe that this 'variant replica' is somewhat later than the ex-Spiridon version and was probably inspired, not by the cartoon or by the original painting, but by another more recent variant. Morelli, who was the first to refute the attribution to Leonardo, put forward [ZBK 1874] the name of Sodoma; A. Venturi [Catalogue, 1893] and Berenson [*Disegni Fiorentini*, 1961] called it simply a copy by Sodoma, one of whose drawings (Windsor) is very close to the painting; Longhi agreed [*Precisioni . . .*, 1928] but Müller-Walde and Clark assigned the painting to Bachiacca, and Sirén, and recently Castelfranco [1956] to Bugiardini: a derivation from Sodoma seems most likely for Leda's figure, the rest might be due to individual phantasy. Other copies or variants, studied in detail by P. d'Ancona [A 1920] and P. della Pergola [*Galleria Borghese*, 1955], belong to the Musées Royaux in Brussels (ascribed to Francabigio and to Puligo by Berenson and Sirén), to the Oppler Collection in Hanover (eighteenth century, according to Müller-Walde), the Pembroke Collection in Wilton House (mentioned by Richardson), the Henry-Doetscher Collection in London (attributed to Giampetrino), the Kaunitz

Drawings possibly connected with 35 (above, and from the left and from the top); Storm over a Valley and a Town (red chalk, 290 × 150 mm.; Windsor, Royal Library); Trees in the Sun (red chalk, 290 × 150; ibid.); Drape over the Virgin's arm (black chalk, red chalk, heightened with white, drawn over a pen on a reddish ground, 85 × 17; ibid.); Draped knee of the Virgin (black chalk, heightened with white, 160 × 145; ibid.). (Below, from left to right) Mountain Range (red chalk on pink ground, detail; ibid.); Composition sketch (pen over black chalk, 122 × 100; Venice, Accademia).

Copies and derivations from 35 (opposite page, from the top), paintings in: Florence (Uffizi; sometimes attributed to Salaino); Madrid (Prado: attributed to Cesare da Sesto by A. Venturi); Milan (Brera); cartoon in Budapest (Szépmüvészeti Muzeum; formerly attributed to Leonardo); another painting in Rome (Tabacchi Collection [?]; attributed to Salaino). (Above, from the top) paintings in: Milan (Poldi Pezzoli Museum; ascribed to Cesare da Sesto); Poznan (National Museum; attributed to Q. Metsys); Chiusa ([Trent], Convent of the Capuchins; by the school of Luini), and (below) Paris (Collection of F. de Rothschild; free version with the young St John, attributed to Luini).

Collection in Vienna (mentioned by Amoretti when it belonged to the Firmian family, in Italy), the Richerton Collection in London, formerly Mattei in Rome [Amoretti], and the J. G. Johnson Collection in Philadelphia (which might be identical with the copy once owned by Barker, in England). A miniature copy on parchment was part of the collection of the Italian art historian P. d'Ancona.

But Leonardo certainly conceived, designed, and perhaps painted another *Leda*, less monumental and more lively, which we know through the autograph drawing in Rotterdam (Boymans Museum) and the one in Chatsworth, which is more vigorous and was once attributed to Sodoma, but is now generally accepted. Sheet No. 12337 r. in Windsor, with two tiny nude women, without eggs and without swan is undoubtedly connected with that *Leda*, which would be later than the standing one – and in fact Berenson dates the three drawings from a later period. A *Leda* by Giampetrino, perhaps the same as in 1806, was in the Kassel gallery and went from there to Malmaison and in 1840 to Wilhelm II of Holland and from him to his heir the Princess of Wied. This picture seems directly connected with the drawings we mentioned; apart from its artistic value, it is the only record in painting of Leonardo's hypothetical second *Leda*.

35  168×112 *1510*

St Anne, The Virgin and the Infant Christ with a Lamb
Paris, Louvre
Leonardo went back to this theme in Florence, even though we must exclude the possibility that the second, lost, cartoon of St Anne with the Virgin, was to be used for the Santissima Annunziata altarpiece. This second cartoon represents a transition between the first one (30) and the painting. The drawing in the Venice Accademia, which Heydenreich dates about 1500 and Popham 1498–9, already bears the germ of this second cartoon, as Pietro da Novellara described it on 3 April 1505, from Florence, to Isabella d'Este: '... [Leonardo] painted a Christ child about one year old, who strains from his mother's arms to grab and hug a lamb. The Virgin, raising herself from St Anne's lap, holds the Child and tries to pull him away from the lamb. St Anne, slightly raising herself, seems to want to prevent her daughter from separating the Child from the lamb.' The Anonimo Gaddiano also mentioned this cartoon: '[Leonardo] made some marvellous drawings, among them a Virgin and a St Anne, who were taken to France'. And Vasari, who had seen neither the cartoon nor the painting, described them brilliantly and in detail: 'At that time [that is, during his stay with the Servite

friars at the Annunziata, as stated in the 1550 edition, and not 'finally', as is said in the 1568 edition] he did a cartoon showing Our Lady with St Anne and the Infant Christ. This work not only won the astonished admiration of all the artists, but when finished, for two days it attracted to the room where it was exhibited a crowd of men and women, young and old, who flocked there as if they were attending a great festival to gaze in amazement at the marvels he had created.' A description follows in which he also mentions 'St John depicted as a little boy playing with a lamb' at the feet of the Virgin, which makes us wonder about the existence of a third cartoon in which he might have used a pyramidal composition with four characters and the lamb. But if this marvellous cartoon is lost, Berenson lists sketches of details which testify to its existence: the Mond drawing at the Metropolitan, in black chalk with touches of colour for the Virgin's head, which looks so finished that it was believed to be a fragment of the cartoon; No. 2257 at the Louvre with the draped legs of the Virgin in black chalk, bistre and white lead. No. 12538 in Windsor Castle in red chalk on red ground, representing the back of the Infant Christ; and also in Windsor, Nos 12526, 12527, 12529, 12530, 12531, 12532, with details of draperies, all in black chalk, heightened with white lead. As for the cartoon owned by Padre Resta, it was like the one belonging to the heirs of Carlo Emanuele di Savoia and mentioned in the 1631 inventory, a good contemporary copy, fitted with two golden shutters which allow us to trace its passing from Marco d'Oggiono (who could even be the author) to a certain Arese, to Bonda, to Resta, to Plattenborg and, in 1830, to Count Esterhazy.

There is no doubt that De Beatis and the Cardinal of Aragon saw the painting in Cloux during their visit of October 1517; but it is equally certain that the King of France did not acquire it and that Melzi could have taken it back to Italy. How Cardinal Richelieu came to find it in Casale Montferrato in 1629–30, during the war for the succession of Mantua, remains a mystery. He gave it to the king in 1636 and it has been in the Louvre since 1810. Some critics claim that the artist was helped by assistants – either by Salai if it was painted during his second stay in Milan, or by Melzi if it was painted in France – arguing that only the landscape, St Anne and the right arm of the Virgin are worthy of Leonardo. The controversies about the possibility of such collaboration have been as long as those about the theological, symbolical and esoteric meanings of the work. According to the technical examination, there was indeed some collaboration

in the application of paint, but the preparatory sketch was entirely by one hand. Recent infra-red photographs taken in the Louvre laboratory have made it possible after five centuries to see, through the coloured strata, the light preparatory sketch by Leonardo. The painting was never finished in some of the details (such as the clothes) and is covered with old restorations and repaintings in less important parts (especially the Virgin's cloak). But all in all it can be considered as autograph. Castelfranco has pointed out the importance of the elaboration and deepening of the theme from the London cartoon to the painting. For our part, we would like to stress the importance of the landscape of abrupt, rocky mountains, of rivers flowing from them to the sea, in an atmosphere muffled by snowflakes and silence: a dreamlike landscape from the world's prehistory. In this geological world which seems to go back to a time when no human life or thought existed, the very leafy tree on the right strikes us as absurdly real, as if it stood there to fix the limit of that primitive chaos. This is an even more deeply symbolical and metaphysical landscape than the background of *The Mona Lisa* (31). There are many total or partial copies of this painting, which exerted a great influence on painters like Raphael, Andrea del Sarto and Michelangelo.

36 177×115 *1511-15

Bacchus Paris, Louvre
Although a Latin distich by Flavio Antonio Giraldi mentions a *Bacchus* painted by Leonardo (probably the one which belonged to Anton Maria Pallavicini from whom the Duke of Ferrara demanded it in 1505), this painting was conceived as a representation of St John the Baptist. Its provenance is almost certainly the collection of François I and it was seen in Fontainebleau by Cassiano del Pozzo [1625]: '... St John in the desert. The figure, less than one third life-size, is a most delicate work, but it does not please much because it does not show any piety and the background is unlikely: the saint is sitting and one can see rocks and an airy green landscape'. (Vatican Library, MS *Barb. lat.* 5688). This description is very detailed and excludes any supposed change of theme. The painting is simply listed as *St John the Baptist in the Desert* by Father Dan [*Trésor*, 1642] and by the Le Brun catalogue [1683], whilst in the Paillet catalogue [1695], the title *St Jean au Désert* is crossed out and replaced by *Bacchus dans un paysage* and, in the margin, a note: 'it was called St John in the old inventories'. When the saint was transformed into a pagan god, probably between 1683 and 1695, the panther skin, the crown of vine-leafs and the grape were added, the

36 Plate LXIV

arrangement of the hair was altered and the cross was changed into a thyrsus. The X-ray examination of the painting made in the Louvre laboratory did not show which part of this work, which comes from Leonardo's workshop, was by the master's hand because the canvas onto which the painting was transferred in the nineteenth century had been treated with lead, which makes it impermeable to X-rays. In addition there is a small red chalk drawing in the Sacro Monte Museum in Varese, in a bad state of preservation, but well finished and representing the same St John; it looks as if it was earlier than the Louvre picture and Tolnay [RV, XIX, 1962] assigns it to Leonardo and dates it, judging by the technique, about 1511–15. If that were the case Leonardo would be responsible for the theme and also for taking part in painting the picture. Waagen attributed the painting to Leonardo and Bernazzano (for the landscape), Frizzoni ascribed the saint to Cesare da Sesto and the landscape to Bernazzano, and so did Sirén (who however, thought that it reproduced a prototype of the master's) and Sudia. Müntz, followed by Jacobsen, thought it was a derivation from Leonardo by Marco d'Oggiono; for Müller-Walde, it was by Francesco Melzi. Most critics now seem to accept the idea of a lost prototype by Leonardo. For our part, we believe that the painting dates from 1511–15 and that there was an original cartoon, now lost, in which the landscape was only vaguely sketched.

A derivation from 36, probably painted by Cesare da Sesto (London [?], Collection of the Earl of Crawford).

St John the Baptist Paris,
Louvre
This is Leonardo's last
masterpiece, entirely by his
hand, fully finished technically,
and almost monochrome.
Frizzoni, Thiis, Reinach,
Müller-Walde and Berenson in
his youth had ascribed it to
Leonardo's school or workshop;
they may have been influenced
by the ambiguous beauty of
this admirable figure, which is
disquietening, half-way
between male and female and
seems the pictorial embodiment
of a strange state of mind. The
atmosphere is dark and clinging.

The painting has a long
history. The Anonimo Gaddiano
only recorded briefly:
'[Leonardo] also painted St
John'. Vasari quotes, among
the pictures belonging to the
Grand Duke Cosimo: 'the head
of an angel, raising one arm so
that it is foreshortened from the
shoulder to the elbow, and
holding the other hand against
his breast' (6) – which seems
an accurate description of *St
John the Baptist*: in that case,
it would have been painted
during the artist's second stay
in Florence. Vasari had a very
good knowledge of the Grand
Duke's collection; but on the
other hand no inventory of the
Medici pictures mentions this
angel. It has been suggested
that the painting derives from
the elaboration of the drawing
of an angel, No. 12328 in
Windsor, dating from about
1506, with one hand pointing
to heaven and the other one
against his breast, but in front
view, in a different position, and
with an expression very far
removed from the indescribable
pathos of *St John*.

Critics agree on dating the
painting either from the last
Roman period, or from the
beginning of Leonardo's stay in
France. Beatis saw it in the
master's studio in Cloux, in
October 1517 and it remained in
France, in the royal collection.
It was not given by Louis XIII to
Charles I of England, as is
commonly believed, but
exchanged against a portrait of
Erasmus by Holbein and a
Holy Family by Titian. When the
royal English collection was
sold after 1649 E. Jabach, a
banker, bought it, and sold it to
Cardinal Mazarin, from whose
heirs (1661) it passed on to
Louis XIV; it went to the
Louvre after the French
revolution. It was submitted to
technical examinations in 1952,
and as a result, it is now
considered the one painting
which is indubitably all by
Leonardo's hand. [RV, XIX, 1962].

*Various copies and derivations
from 37 (from the top),
paintings in: Milan (Ambrosiana;
usually attributed to Salaino;
with a mountain landscape
derived from 35); Paris
(Chéramy Collection); Genoa
(Palazzo Rosso; formerly
attributed to Leonardo, but
probably later); Basle
(Offentliche Kunstsammlung).*

37 Plate LX

Other works sometimes attributed to Leonardo

*The various theories about
Leonardo's activities as a
painter did not come to an
end at the beginning of the
present century. Every year,
critics or amateurs 'launch'
some new discovery which the
press announces with
editorial flourishes, and which,
very often, merely sinks into
oblivion. It is impossible to
mention them all – it would be
difficult enough to keep up with
the various new Mona Lisas
which keep appearing
monotonously. Even if we limit
ourselves to the opinions of
famous art historians, the
material is abundant enough, as
can be seen from the length of
this appendix, in which we have
listed chronologically (taking
up again some facts mentioned
in the Outline Biography
[pp 83–6]) the documentation
which gave rise to some modern
less authoritative or less
persistent attributions.*

*As works at first attributed to
the master are often referred
later to one or the other of his
followers, we give a short list of
the artists concerned.*

**Giovanni Antonio
Boltraffio** (Milan, 1467–1516)
He first painted in the style of
B. Zenale and V. Foppa, then
came to Milan and became one
of Leonardo's earliest and most
faithful disciples.

Cesare da Sesto (Sesto
Calende [Varese], 1477 –
Milan, 1523)
During his first Roman period,
he followed Peruzzi's
Raphaelesque style. Then, in
Milan, he was among
Leonardo's late followers and
tried to translate the master's
inspiration into a monumental
style. Finally, he lived in
southern Italy (1514–20) and
turned to a sort of disorganized
eclecticism.

Bernardino de' Conti (Pavia,
1450–1525 or 28)
He was probably trained by
V. Civerchio and V. Foppa, then
became a close, but somewhat
dry, follower of Leonardo.

Francesco Napoletano
(sixteenth century)
Nothing is known of his life. In
some works ascribed to him by
Morelli, the influence of
Leonardo seems tempered by
that of De Predis.

**Giovanni Ambrogio de
Predis** (Milan, ca 1455 – ca
1508)
He was the pupil and assistant
of his brother Cristoforo, a
miniaturist (1474). In 1482, he
joined the painters of the Milan
court. The following year, he
offered hospitality to Leonardo
and became one of his close
followers.

**Giampetrino (Giovanni
Pedrini,** known as) (Milan,
first half of the sixteenth
century)

He may have been a pupil of
Leonardo's and certainly
imitated his use of *chiaroscuro*
figures against a very dark
background.

Bernardino Luini (?, ca
1480–90 – Milan, 1532)
He was first connected with
Ambrogio da Fossano, known
as Borgognone. He then came
under the stylistic influence of
Solario, Bramantino and above
all Leonardo. He painted
peaceful, idyllic narrative
paintings with a personal touch
of clarity, particularly in the
landscapes and in the languid
grace of the polished figures.

**The Master of the Sforza
Altarpiece** (fifteenth
century)
The name comes from an
altarpiece representing the
Virgin and Child enthroned,

*The so-called Sforza altarpiece
(Milan, Brera).*

two angels, four saints and
Lodovico il Moro and his court
as worshippers. It was painted
about 1495 for Sant'Ambrogio
ad Nemus in Milan and is now
in the Brera. The artist allies the
style of V. Foppa with iconographic and expressive elements
borrowed from Leonardo.

Cesare Magni (Milan,
sixteenth century)
Among the late disciples of the
master, he stands out for his
disorganised compositions and
his porcelain-like colours.

Marco da Oggiono (Oggiono
[Como] ?, ca 1475–1530)
Throughout his whole life, he
was a faithful, but modest
follower of Leonardo, and
probably his pupil.

Francesci Melzi (Milan, ca
1493 – Vaprio d'Adda [Milan],
ca 1570)
He was a pupil of Leonardo and
accompanied him to Rome and
to Amboise. He inherited his
manuscripts, and imitated his
style faithfully, but coldly.

Salaino (Andrea Caprotti,
known as) (?, 1480 – Milan,
ca 1524–34)
He was Leonardo's favourite
pupil. No documented
paintings by his hand survived.

In the few works which are
ascribed to him, he shows a
looser style than his master,
with a thin, uncertain *sfumato*.

**Sodoma (Giovanni
Antonio Bazzi,** known as)
Vercelli, 1477 – Siena, 1549)
To the influence of his master,
G. M. Spanzotti, he added
elements derived from
Perugino and Raphael. After
coming in contact with
Leonardo's painting, his own
refined eclecticism was
indelibly marked by the
master's influence.

Andrea Solario (Milan, ca
1460 – ca 1520)
He was the brother, and pupil
of the sculptor and
architect Cristoforo Solario.
From 1503 onwards, he was
strongly influenced by
Leonardo (*Crucifixion*, Paris,
Louvre). But later, Venetian and
Flemish elements were added.

1478
38 and 39 Two Virgins
'[. . .]ber 1478, I began the two
pictures of the Virgin Mary':
this note by Leonardo's hand on
sheet No. 446 in the Uffizi has
given rise to numerous
hypotheses. Some art
historians connect it with the
*Madonna with the Vase of
Flowers* (12) and with the lost
Madonna della Caraffa, once
belonging to Clement VII (56),
with the one for Giovanni Botti
described by Bocchi, and with
the lost *Madonna with the Cat*
and also *The Benois Madonna*
(9). These are labours lost,
since the two heads drawn on
the same sheet are male (one
old, one young) and there is no
way of tying that note to any
given works. (See also 10).

ca **1482**
**40 Portrait of Cecilia
Gallerani**
None of the known portraits has
been definitely proved to be that
of the mistress of Lodovico il
Moro. The girl in the Cracow
portrait (27) does not seem 'of
so immature an age' as to
justify the remark in Cecilia
Gallerani's letter to Isabella
d'Este (see also 26 and 102).

1485
41 Madonna for Matthias
Corvinus
If Lodovico il Moro's
instructions to his
ambassador in Budapest,
Maffeo Trevigliese, concern
Leonardo, as we suppose, the
artist received a commission
from the duke for a *Madonna*
for the King of Hungary
(Outline Biography **1485**).
Nothing more is known of this
possible work or its execution.

ca **1496**
**42 Portrait of Lucrezia
Crivelli**
As in the case of Cecilia
Gallerani, there is no proof that
any one of the existing portraits
is that of Lodovico's last
favourite (cf. 28).

1505
43 Bacchus
On 1 April the Duke of Ferrara
expressed to Seregno, his agent,
the desire of acquiring a

Drawing (pen, 202 × 268 mm.; Florence, Uffizi) with the important autograph note about the two pictures of the Virgin Mary (38 and 39). The two profiles facing each other, one old and one young, have been connected with The Adoration of the Magi (14): the young one corresponds in the painting to the upturned face on the right; the other sketches represent pieces of machinery like those on the back of the sheet.

Studies for a Virgin worshipping the Child (pen over lead paint on pink ground, 195 × 170 mm.; New York, Metropolitan Museum), probably earlier than 1480 and therefore possibly connected with 38 and 39. But they are usually considered as preparatory sketches for a Nativity which was never executed and which seems to have occupied Leonardo's mind even before he started work on The Adoration of the Magi.

Bacchus by Leonardo, which then belonged to A. M. Pallavicini, and on 27 of that month, Seregno communicated the regrets of the owner, who had already promised the painting to the Cardinal of Rouen. This was probably the same Bacchus mentioned in a Latin distich by Flavio Antonio Giraldi in a manuscript in the Ferrara Library, dating from about 1550 [Campori, 1865; Beltrami, Documenti, 1919].

1507
44 Madonna (?)
From a letter dated 12 January, by Francesco Pandolfini, the ambassador of the Signoria at the French court, we learn that the King of France already

owned a small painting by Leonardo. It might have been the original of The Virgin with the Yarn Winder, painted for Robertet (32). As for the 'small pictures of Our Lady' and others, mentioned later, which the king wanted to commission from him (Outline Biography), we know that Leonardo was working on an altarpiece when he had to go back to Florence to settle the lawsuit against his brothers. It is also likely that the painter was referring to the king's commission in his 1507 letter (ibid.).

A letter from Charles d'Amboise to the Signoria in Florence, on 15 August (see Critical History) makes it clear that when Leonardo left Milan he had interrupted the painting

of an altarpiece for the king 'who valued it greatly'. Since there is no other reference to this work, it might possibly have been the second version of The Virgin of the Rocks (15 and 16).

ca 1510
45 and 46 Two Madonnas
In the rough copies of two letters, possibly to the Governor of Milan, written from Florence ('I have almost settled the law suit against my brothers'), Leonardo promises to return to Milan for Easter bringing back 'two pictures of Our Lady, of different sizes . . . which are intended for our most Christian King . . .' (Codex Atl. 317 r., 372 v.). The date is uncertain and there are no other documents or notes to confirm this statement.

1517
47 Female Portrait
The portrait of 'a certain Florentine lady, painted on the request of the late Giuliano de' Medici' was seen in that year at Cloux by the Cardinal of Aragon and mentioned by Antonio de Beatis. The identification with The Mona Lisa (31) is probable, but not certain. Among the property left to Melzi in his will, Leonardo particularly mentioned several 'portraits' which means that the portrait in question was not the only one he had with him in France.

1520
48 Female Portrait
Enea Irpino, a poet from Parma, wrote sonnets and ballads [Canzoniere, 1520] in praise of a painting by Leonardo. The anonymous sitter may have been, according to Pezzana [1827] in his appendix to Affò [Memorie dei letterati parmigiani, 1791] Isabel of Aragon, and the painting, The Lady with the Pearl Hair-net (26). B. Croce [Canzoniere d'amore per Costanza d'Avalos duchessa di Francavilla, in Aneddoti di varia letteratura, 1953] asserted that the lady was Constanza d'Avalos and wrote two sonnets and two madrigals in which the name of Vinci is repeated three times [AAP 1903].

1531
49 Lady with Dishevelled Hair
A painting given by Count

D. de' Conti (?): Portrait of a Young Woman (Washington, National Gallery [Kress]), formerly attributed to Leonardo by some critics and connected with 47.

Niccia Mattei to the royal palace in Mantua. It may be the same which is described in the 1627 inventory of the Gonzaga Collection as: 'Portrait of a woman with dishevelled hair, a sketch in a frame, by Leonardo da Vinci, 1,803 lire [a very high price]'. (see 17).

1536
50 Self-portrait (?)
At that date a relative of Leonardo's presented Cardinal Salviati with a portrait painted by the master, according to a note by B. Oltrocchi in the Vinci archive, mentioned by Amoretti who links it with a so-called self-portrait of Leonardo in the house of the Nicolini in Florence. But even the original note is doubtful in its substance.

1542–7
51–4 Madonna – St John The Baptist – Altarpiece – Portrait of Pier Francesco del Giocondo
The Anonimo Gaddiano mentions, apart from the works which were later recorded by Vasari: a painting on wood representing 'Our Lady, a most excellent work'; a St John the Baptist which, from the context, does not appear to be the one in the Louvre (37); an altarpiece sent by Lodovico il Moro to the Emperor of Germany, which does not tally with the first version of The Virgin of the Rocks (15) and The Portrait of Pier Francesco del Giocondo (see also 31).

1543
55 Madonna nursing the Child
'In the house of M. Michiel Contarini, near the Misericordia . . . there is a small painting of one foot [high (?)], or a little more [ca 30 cm], coloured by the hand of Leonardo Vinci', so wrote Marcantonio Michiel. It is possible that Leonardo had left behind a work of his after his stay in Venice, but the hypothesis according to which this Madonna is the one now in Leningrad (18) has very little foundation,

1550
56 Madonna della Caraffa
A picture recorded by Vasari as having belonged to Pope Clement VII. It has been tentatively identified with the Munich Madonna (12) without any documentary evidence (see also 38, 39 and 100).

1568
57 and 58 Laughing Lady – St John the Baptist
Both pictures are recorded by Vasari in the Mint in Milan. There is no particular reason to identify 58 with the Louvre picture (37).

59 and 60 Virgin holding the Child in her Arms – Portrait of a Child
Recorded in Pescia by Vasari as works executed by Leonardo during his stay in Rome for Baldassarre Turini from Pescia, the datary of Leo X. All the works collected by Turini have been lost.

Portrait of a Lady (drawing; Florence, Uffizi), long believed to be by Leonardo's hand, but probably by one of his followers (see 48).

So-called Self-portrait by Leonardo (Cherbourg, Hôtel de Ville): one of the many which might fit the 1536 document (50).

St John the Baptist (Rome, Galleria Borghese), believed to be a copy from an original by Leonardo (see 52).

Giampetrino, Madonna nursing the Child (Rome, Galleria Borghese), one of the many works on that theme which were attributed to Leonardo (55).

Fight between a Dragon and a Lion, *drawing (Florence, Uffizi), formerly considered by Leonardo's hand, but probably a copy, possibly of the lost 62.*

1569
61 Judith
Cardinal Ippolito d'Este sent from Rome to the Duke of Ferrara a picture unknown there (Modena, *Archivio di Stato*) ; it could be the 'Judith by Lunardo da Vinci' listed in an inventory of works restored by Bastiano Filippi Vecchio for a small chapel belonging to the duchess. [A. Venturi, ASA 1888].

1584
62 Dragon and Lion fighting
'[Leonardo] painted a dragon fighting with a lion, with such skill . . . I once owned a sketch of that picture which I valued very much' [Lomazzo, *Trattato*]. There is a drawing on that subject in the Uffizi, which Suida considers as a copy from an original by Leonardo.

1589
63 Head of St John the Baptist
This picture is mentioned by Borghini *Il Riposo* in the house of Camillo degli Albizzi, and in a poem by Tasso dedicated to the same Camillo. But the head published by Luigi Albizzi in 1919 as a picture in his palace in Fiesole and a work by Leonardo is much later in date, according to A. Venturi [1920].

64 Head of a Dead Man
Borghini remembered having seen that picture in the villa *Il Riposo* belonging to B. Vecchietti, near Ponte a Ema; there is no other record of it.

1590
65 Pomona
Recorded by Lomazzo [*Idea del Tempio della pittura*] : 'A laughing Pomona partly covered by three veils – which is a very difficult thing to represent – by Leonardo who painted it for François I, King of France'. There is no trace of that work : Lomazzo mentions it either from hearsay, or because of a supposed copy.

1591
66 Madonna
Mentioned by Bocchi [*Bellezze della città di Firenze*] in the house of the Botti family. There is no trace of that painting.

ante **1600**
67–70 The Four Seasons – Portrait of Pico Della Mirandola – Portrait of a Young Man from the Visconti – Sleeping Woman
Those pictures were attributed

Two Heads of St John the Baptist *attributed to A. Solario (Paris, Louvre; and Milan, Gallarati Scotti Collection) and tentatively connected with 63. (Below, from the top) possible derivations from 71: Marco da Oggiono, The Redeemer (Rome, Galleria Borghese; Cesare da Sesto (?), The Redeemer (Milan, Trivulzio Collection).*

to Leonardo in the inventory of the collection of Fulvio Orsini, who died in 1600 [P. de Nolhac, GBA 1884] (see also 22 and 23).

1611
71 The Redeemer blessing
Such a painting in oils was presented by Pope Paul V to Scipione Borghese as from the hand of Leonardo. It is now in the Galleria Borghese in Rome where it was attributed to Leonardo throughout the nineteenth century until Lübcke [*Geschichte der italienischen Malerei . . .*, 1878] suggested it was a school work ; then Morelli [1897] assigned it to Marco da Oggiono. About the middle of the seventeenth century, W. Hollar published an engraving on the same subject, claiming it as a copy after an original by Leonardo ; a painting connected with the print was found a few years ago in a Milan private collection and attributed to Leonardo by Coletti, but without proof.
Wirckelmann also alluded to a *Head of the Redeemer* [*Storia delle arti del disegno*, 1768] in the Liechtenstein Collection. Other similar works have been attributed to Leonardo, but modern art historians have in every case denied those attributions.

1624
72 Virgin with the Infant Christ and an Angel
There is an entry in the inventory of the collection of Cardinal Alessandro d'Este [Campori, *Raccolta di cataloghi*, 1870] : 'Madonna, infant Christ and angel on wood, with gilded frame, by Leonardo da Vinci'.

1625
73 The Rape of Proserpina
Cassiano del Pozzo saw a painting on this subject, 'most skilled but somewhat dry', in Fontainebleau.

1626
74 Christ among the Doctors
It was mentioned as a work by Leonardo in the inventory as in the possession of Olimpia Aldobrandini in Rome [Della Pergola, in Davies, 1961] and quoted as such by Leonetti and Chigi. Amoretti [1804] records that it was sold to an Englishman, Mr Day, who did in fact acquire the picture in 1800–1. It passed through various hands and was finally bought by the National Gallery in London, where it is rightly attributed to Luini.

1649
75 Portrait of Colombine
A portrait on that subject was listed as a work of Leonardo in the collection of Marie de' Medici in Paris ; it later belonged to the Duke of Orléans; in 1792 it was sold for 6,500 francs to Udney, then passed through the hands of Walckiers, a Brussels banker, of Danoot, and finally of William II of Holland, with whose collection it was bought by the Hermitage museum for 81,200 francs in 1850. In 1891,

Somoff attributed it to Luini. Morelli ascribes it to Giampetrino and Cavalcaselle to Solario. Francesco Melzi seems the most likely of all the artists suggested.

1650
76 Saint Catherine
Ferdinando II of Tuscany and the Duke of Modena, Francesco I d'Este exchanged two paintings (Modena, *Archivio Estense*) : one on that theme, attributed to Leonardo, and a Titan portrait [A. Venturi,

B. Luini: Christ among the Doctors (London, National Gallery) (see 74).

(From the top) F. Melzi (?): Colombine (Leningrad, Hermitage); B. Luini, Young Woman (see 75). (Below) B. Luini: St Catherine (Rome, Galleria Borghese) (76).

La Galleria Estense, 1882]. The *St Catherine* is listed in the duke's collection by Scannelli [*Microscosmo*, 1657]. It is almost certainly a work by Luini or one of his followers, but it has not been identified.

1651
77 Portrait of a Young Lady
This picture was in the collection of Charles I of England, which was sold in 1651. It entered the Dutch De Vries Collection as a Holbein (1738 sale). It was again attributed to Leonardo in the collection of William II of Holland in the Hague and was listed as such by Amoretti. It now belongs to the Mauritshuis (No. 275) at The Hague and is ascribed to Holbein the Younger.

1657
78 Young Man in Armour
Mentioned by Scannelli [*Microcosmo*] as belonging to the Duke of Modena. There is no record of it and it is almost certainly a wrong attribution.

1657
79 Portrait of Joan of Aragon
A 'portrait from nature of queen Joan in Naples' is mentioned in Rome, also by Scannelli, in the Aldobrandini Collection. In the Galleria Borghese, there is a *Woman's Head* (a drawing in silver point) once attributed to Leonardo, which may be by the 'Master of the Sforza altarpiece' and the *Redeemer blessing* by Marco da Oggiono (71) ; in the Doria-Pamphili Collection, an old copy of *Joan of Aragon* by Raphael's workshop, which might also have been attributed to Leonardo (see 106). But the so-called *Queen Joan* is almost certainly the *Portrait of a Lady* sold by the Aldobrandini family to the Leyland Collection, then to the Benson Collection (1894) and finally to the National Gallery of Art in Washington, as Luini's most famous portrait [Ottino della Chiesa, *Luini*, 1956].

1659
80 Herodias
This picture is listed both in the inventory (1659) of the collection of Leopold Wilhelm of Austria (No. 429), and in Teniers' *Theatrum pictoricum* (1660). It was acquired as a Leonardo by the Vienna Museum, where, in 1882, it was attributed to Luini by Engert and called *Salome*. This attribution is now generally accepted [Ottino della Chiesa, *Luini*, 1956]

1664
81 Madonna and Donor
This is a lunette painted in fresco in the cloister of Sant' Onofrio in Rome. According to Muñoz, the donor can be identified with Francesco Cabañas, Chancellor to Alexander II. G. Averi was the first to ascribe it to Leonardo [*Roma in ogni stato*] and this was accepted by Titi, Resta, Pancirolo-Pusteria, Lanzi, D. Agincourt and Müntz [1899]. Reymond attributed it to Cesare da Sesto and Suida

B. Luini; Portrait of a Lady (Washington, National Gallery), possibly connected with 79.

B. Luini; Salome (Vienna, Kunsthistorisches Museum; detail) (see 80).

Cesare da Sesto (?): Madonna and Donor (Rome, Cloister of Sant' Onofrio) (81).

R. del Ghirlandaio; Portrait of a Goldsmith (Florence, Pitti) (82). (Below) Virgin with the Scales (Paris, Louvre) (83).

followed, with reservations. Morelli, and after him Frizzoni, Carotti, A. Venturi and various other critics ascribed it to Boltraffio.

1668
82 Portrait of a Goldsmith
Cardinal Leopoldo de' Medici acquired the picture from Paolo da Sera as a Leonardo, and it was placed in the Galleria Palatina under that description. The attribution remained unchallenged until Morelli [1897] rightly ascribed it to Ridolfo del Ghirlandaio. He was followed by A. Venturi [1924] whilst Suida [1929] attributed it to Francabigio.

1678
83 Virgin with the Scales
This picture was sold to Louis XIV by the Marquis de Béthune for 4,000 *écus*, as a work by Leonardo, and was listed as such in the Louvre (No. 1604). Waagen attributed it to Marco da Oggiono; Passavant to Salaino; Seidlitz to the young Luini; Mündler, Morelli, Berenson, Frizzoni, Reymond and Suida to Cesare da Sesto.

1680
84 Virgin with St John and St Jerome
Listed as a work by Leonardo in the inventory of the Palazzo del Giardino in Parma [Campori, 1870]. It then passed into the Capodimonte Museum where it was attributed to Leonardo's school until Sangiorgi's catalogue [1852]. It has now been suggested that the author may be Giampetrino.

85 St Jerome
This picture was mentioned in the same inventory, also as a work by Leonardo. There are no later records of the painting, which is certainly not the one now in the Pinacoteca Vaticana. (13; see also 103).

1691
86 Virgin with the Child holding a Lily
Engraved by Juster (1691) from the alleged original in the Patin Collection in Paris, with the following inscription in Latin: 'Jesus playing in the lap of his Holy Mother, holding a lily. The perfect work of Leonardo da Vinci for his very Christian Majesty, François I'. From the copy – one of forty, which are badly drawn and engraved – in *Tabellae selectae Carolinae Patinae*, the original from which it was made cannot have been by Leonardo. Suida dates the lost Leonardo original about 1490.

1710
87 Holy Family with St Michael and Andrew
This picture was in the Galleria Sanvitale in Parma, attributed to Leonardo both in the manuscript catalogue by Padre Orlandi (estimated at 2,000 *scudi*), and in another catalogue from the beginning of the nineteenth century (30,000 *lire*). Sanvitale acquired it from the church of the Annunziata in Parma on 11 November 1706 with a false signature 'Leonardo da Vinci

Giampietrino, Virgin with St John and St Jerome (Naples, Capodimonte Museum), see 84.

Giampietrino (?), Virgin with the Child holding a Lily (Gloucester, Highnam Court) 86.

Study of a lily – *pen and watercolour on charcoal (Windsor, Royal Library) unanimously considered to be autograph; possibly related to* 86. *(Below) Cima da Conegliano, The Holy Family with St Michael and St Andrew (Parma, National Gallery)* 87.

1492'. It was considered as genuine by Amoretti, Rio and the painter Gaetano Callani. Transferred to the Galleria Nazionale in Parma in 1834, it was ascribed to Cima da Conegliano (as one of his earliest works, about 1510) by Cavalcaselle, and in the Martini catalogue [1875, No. 361].

1734
88 Half-length figure feeding a kitten
Mentioned in the collection of Cardinal Ruffo, bishop of Ferrara [Agnelli, Catalogue, 1734].

1756
89 Pomona and Vertumnus
This picture was attributed to Leonardo in Oesterreichs' catalogue of the museum of Sans Souci in Potsdam. From there it went to the Berlin Gallery and was attributed to Francesco Melzi in 1830. Mariette [*Abecadario* III] saw a *Pomona and Vertumnus* which seems identical in the Saint-Simon Collection, signed by Melzi. But unlike the Berlin one, the Pomona was nude (see also 65).

1766
90 Christ in the House of Martha and Mary
Engraved by Sentner from an alleged original which was then in Sans Souci, Potsdam.

1770
91 Modesty and Vanity
Formerly in the Barberini Collection in Rome, it was engraved by Volpato as a work by Leonardo. It was then acquired by the Sciarra Colonna family and entailed as a Leonardo in 1818. Prince Maffeo Barberini Sciarra Colonna took it to Paris and sold it to Rothschild, in whose collection it has remained to this day. The author was in fact Bernardino Luini [Ottino della Chiesa, *Luini*, 1956].

1775
92 St Sebastian
Mentioned in the catalogue of the famous Crozat Collection in Paris. It then went to Dubois, a Turin dealer, and was sold as a Leonardo for 100,000 francs to Cavaliere Bistoli, in Rome. It later belonged to Wolsey Moreau, and finally went to the Hermitage in Leningrad. It is a dated work by Bernardino Luini [Ottino della Chiesa, *Luini*, 1956].

1775
93 Holy Family with St Catherine
This painting was acquired by the Abate Salvadori as a Leonardo, and sold as such by his heirs to Catherine of Russia for the Hermitage Museum [Waagen, 1863]. It is now attributed to Cesare da Sesto.

94 St Helena
Ascribed to Leonardo in the inventory of the Boschi Collection in Bologna [Campori].

1780
95 Madonna nursing the Child
The Grand Duke of Tuscany bought this picture from the

Ill-assorted Couple (drawing, Vienna, Albertina), probably a composition made up from various drawings by Leonardo (see 88).

F. Melzi: Pomona and Vertumnus (Berlin, Staatliche Museen) (89).

B. Luini: Modesty and Vanity (Pregny, collection of M. Rothschild) (91); sometimes interpreted as Mary and Martha. A similar work, perhaps also by Luini, is in the San Diego Art Gallery (California). (Below) B. Luini: St Sebastian (Leningrad, Hermitage) (92).

church of S. Michele di Castello di Quarto for 500 *scudi* [Repetti] ; it is now in the reserve of the Florence museums. It cannot be identified with 55.

1784
96 Virgin standing with the Child in her Arms
This picture belongs to the Spanish royal family. It first appeared, as a Leonardo, in the Pourtalès sale of 1865 (83,500 francs) [Mireur, II]. It is a variant or a copy of *The Virgin standing with the Child*

Cesare da Sesto: Holy Family with St Catherine (*Leningrad, Hermitage*) (*93*).

B. Luini: Salome with the Head of St John the Baptist (*Madrid, Prado*) (*97*).

B. Luini: Child playing Patience (*Peterborough, Proby Collection*) (*98*). (*Below*) *B. Luini:* Virgin and Child, standing (*Naples, Capodimonte*) (*99*).

by Luini, in the Hermitage Museum [Ottino della Chiesa, *Luini*, 1956] (see 104).

1793
97 The Executioner offering the Head of St John the Baptist to Salome
This painting was bought by the Uffizi, from Vienna, attributed to Leonardo. It is a work by Luini, and there are other variants, all with half-length figures [Ottino della Chiesa, *Luini*, 1956].

1801
98 Child playing Patience
While in the famous Arundel Collection, this picture was engraved – as a Leonardo – by F. Bartolozzi. As such, it was sold to Lord Hamilton and passed through several hands. Later it was acquired by Lord Carysford (1889). On the occasion of a London exhibition at the Burlington Gallery (1899), A. Venturi rightly attributed it to Luini. With that attribution, it is now in the Proby Collection in Peterborough.

1802
99 Virgin and Child, standing
In that year it belonged, as a Leonardo, to the Francavilla Gallery in Naples. It was later acquired by the Capodimonte Gallery and was rightly ascribed to Luini by Sangiorgi. There are replicas by Luini himself in the Dijon Museum and in the Prentiss Collection in Cleveland (USA).

1804
100 Virgin and Child with the Young St John
This tondo was acquired as a Leonardo by the Galleria Borghese in Rome, from the Salviati family. It was identified by Amoretti and others as *The Madonna* once belonging to Clement VII and mentioned by Vasari (see 56). It is now rightly ascribed to Lorenzo di Credi [Della Pergola, Catalogue, 1959].

101 St Catherine between two Young Angels
This picture is a late copy after Luini, which Amoretti mentions as belonging to the painter Appiani. It is now in the Brera in Milan. The best version has been in the Hermitage in Leningrad since 1814 and came, from the collection of Empress Josephine at Malmaison. A variant, formerly in the Mond Collection, is now in the National Gallery in London. There are copies in Compiègne and Bilbao [Ottino della Chiesa, *Luini*, 1956] (see also 76).

1804
102 Portrait of Cecilia Gallerani
The sitter is represented holding 'with one hand a fold of her garment'. For Amoretti, who mentions it in the Pallavicini house in Milan, this is an undoubted work by Leonardo (see 40).

1805
103 St Jerome
This picture came to London, from the Barberini sale as a Leonardo (11,570 francs) [Mireur]. It is the *St Jerome*

sitting under a Tree in the Cook Collection attributed to Cesare da Sesto or to Bernazzano by Suida, who connects it with the drawing of a head in the Albertina in Vienna (see also 85).

1811
104 Virgin standing with the Child in her Arms
This picture was acquired in Rome as a Leonardo by Count Italinsky and went to the Hermitage Museum under that attribution. It is one of the most typical Luini madonnas

Lorenzo di Credi: Virgin with the Child and the Young St John (*Rome, Galleria Borghese*) (*100*). (*Below*) *B. Luini:* St Catherine (*Leningrad, Hermitage*) (*101*).

Cesare da Sesto and C. Bernazzano (?): St Jerome (*Formerly Richmond, Cook Collection*) (*103*). (*Below*) *B. Luini:* Virgin and Child (*Leningrad, Hermitage*) (*104*).

[Ottino della Chiesa, *Luini*, 1956] (see also 96).

105 Female Portrait
This picture came to London after the Duke of San Pietro sale (78,000 francs) [Mireur]. Nothing is known of it since then.

1819
106 Portrait of Joan of Aragon
This picture was listed in the Belli inventory of the Doria-Pamphili Gallery and was examined on the request of Cardinal Pacca. The verdict was 'a painting on wood representing Queen Joan, by Leonardo da Vinci'. It is a copy contemporary with *Joan of Aragon*, by Raphael's workshop, in the Louvre. It still belongs to the Doria-Pamphili Collection.

1819
107 Virgin and Child (*Il Madonnone*)
This fresco with whole-length figures was formerly under the colonnade (now in the museum) of the Villa Melzi in Vaprio d'Adda. It was attributed to the master by S. Ticozzi [GM 1819], followed by Mongeri (but only the upper part, which is reproduced here) ASL 1885 and F. Melzi d'Eril [*La Madonna di Leonardo . . .*, 1895]. But already then I. Fumagalli [*La Scuola di Leonardo*, 1811] attributed it to Leonardo's circle, and so have most modern critics, including Suida [1929] who suggested the 'Master of St Euphemia'. Morelli ascribed it to Sodoma and dated it about 1518–21 but Cust has rejected that attribution [1906].

1827
108 The Virgin between St Barbara and St Catherine
This picture was engraved by J. Steinmüller as a work by Leonardo. It then belonged to the collection of Prince Esterhazy. It is now in the Budapest Museum where it is still attributed to Leonardo although Kugler [*Handbuch der Kunstgeschichte*, 1861] has definitively ascribed it to Luini.

1847
109 Virgin and Child with St Jerome and Peter
Listed as a work by Leonardo in the catalogue of the famous Solly Collection in Berlin. It passed through the Crivelli Collection in Milan, then in the Cook Collection in Richmond. Ascribed to Cesare Magni.

1855
110 Salome
Auctioned as a Leonardo in the Callot sale (16,500 francs) [Mireur]. It is certainly one of Luini's variants on this theme or on the similar theme of Herodias (see 80 and 97).

1864
111 Portrait of a Young Man
In the Hermitage Museum, Leningrad. Waagen was the first to attribute it to Leonardo. But Hark [1896] attributed it to Boltraffio.

112 Portrait of a Nude Woman
Also in the Hermitage and also ascribed to Leonardo by Waagen, but with no following even at the time. There are other copies, the most famous of which is in the Casa Primoli in Rome, where it was mentioned by De Rinaldis [1926].

1871
113 Virgin and Child with the Young St John
From the Woodburne Collection, this picture went to the Dresden Museum in 1860, attributed

Raphael Workshop: Portrait of Joan of Aragon (*Rome, Palazzo Doria*) (*106*).

School of Leonardo: Il Madonnone (*Vaprio d'Adda, Villa Melzi*) (*107*).

B. Luini: The Virgin between St Barbara and St Catherine (*Budapest, Szépmüvészeti Muzeum*) (*108*). (*Below*) *Lorenzo di Credi:* Virgin with the Child and the Young St John (*Dresden, Gemäldegalerie*) (*113*).

School of Leonardo: Christ resurrected with St Leonard and St Lucy (*Berlin, Staatliche Museen*) (*114*).

Cesare da Sesto: The Virgin enthroned with two Saints (*New York, S. H. Kress Foundation*) (*115*). *A work of high quality, as has been shown by a careful restoration which revealed some interesting alterations in the painting.*

Virgin with the Castle (*Private Collection*) (*117*). (*Below, from the left*) Leonardo: St Sebastian (*lightly drawn in black chalk, 145 × 55 mm.; Bayonne, Musée Bonnat*). *School of Leonardo:* St Sebastian (*Brescia, Pinacoteca*) (*118*).

---

to Lorenzo di Credi. Hübner then ascribed it to Leonardo's first Florentine period [1871], followed by Colvin [BM 1911]. Other critics disagreed ; but the present attribution is still the original one to Lorenzo di Credi, which was established again in 1877 through the Woermann catalogue [Dalli Regoli, 1966].

1884
114 Christ resurrected with St Leonard and St Lucy
Originally in the church of Sta Liberata in Milan where it was attributed to Bramantino. It later belonged to the Solly Collection and to the Berlin museums (1821). According to Waagen — and this is the most acceptable opinion — it is a work by Leonardo's school. Bode ascribed it to Leonardo [1884] and Suida accepted that attribution, and later [1929] admitted the possibility of workshop collaboration.

1888
115 Virgin and Child enthroned between St John the Baptist and St George
(*The Virgin with the Bas Relief*)
This picture was formerly in the church of S. Domenico in Messina. It was bought by Lord Haston, a minister of Ferdinand IV of Bourbon. It passed through the Warwick and the Gatton collections, as a Leonardo. In 1888 it was sold for 63,000 francs [Mireur] to the Cook Collection in Richmond and was again ascribed, rightly, to Cesare da Sesto, about 1520. It now belongs to the Kress Foundation in New York.

1891
116 Virgin and Child with a Lamb
From the Habich Collection in Cassel, this picture went, as a Leonardo, to the Brera in Milan, for the price of 8,500 *lire*. It comes from the Borghese family in Rome and later belonged to the Ropp Collection in Cologne. It was inspired by *St Anne* in the Louvre (35), like the other replicas exhibited in London in 1899. It was first attributed to a possible collaboration between Leonardo and Sodoma and later ascribed, with reservations, to the latter [Cust, 1906].

1929
117 Virgin with the Castle
In a private collection. Ascribed to Leonardo by Suida (but his attribution has not been accepted).

118 St Sebastian
This picture belongs to the Brescia Pinacoteca. It was also ascribed to Leonardo by Suida, but the attribution seems even less likely than 117.

119 Virgin with the Child who stretches his hands towards a cup.
From the Szépmüvészeti Muzeum in Budapest. Suida, who first attributed it to Leonardo, later rightly ascribed it to Boltraffio.

G. A. Boltraffio: Virgin and Child (*Budapest, Szépmüvészeti Muzeum*) (*119*)

G. A. Boltraffio: Virgin and Child picking a Flower (*Milan, Poldi Pezzoli Museum*) (*120*). *This work is considered one of the best by Boltraffio. The rich, enamel-like paint is consistent with his style about the end of the fifteenth century.*

School of Leonardo: St Anne, the Virgin and the Child with a Lamb (*Paris, Louvre*) (*121*). (*Below*) School of Leonardo: The Virgin with the Child and the Young St John playing (*London, Harris Collection*) (*122*).

---

120 Virgin and Child
This picture in the Poldi Pezzoli Museum in Milan has been constantly and correctly attributed to Boltraffio since 1881, except by Suida who believes it to be the result of a collaboration between Leonardo and Boltraffio.

121 St Anne, the Virgin and the Child with a Lamb
In the Louvre. According to Suida, it is entirely the work of Leonardo. In fact it is one of the many school variants of the well-known Louvre picture of the same subject (35).

1930
122 Virgin with the Child and the Young St John playing
This copy of a painting reproducing the drawing by Leonardo in the Metropolitan Museum in New York was discovered in the reserve of the Uffizi by Müller [1929]. The latter supposes that the lost original could be by Cesare da Sesto and connects it with Leonardo's note of 1508 about two Madonnas. Borenius mentions another version in the Harris Collection in London [BM 1930], as the original.

1939
123 Madonna with the Cat
During the Leonardo exhibition in Milan, it was believed that the original of this picture had been discovered in the Noya Collection from Savona. But in fact the work is a late conflation made up from the master's drawings (see also 8).

1957
124 Virgin worshipping the Child, and two Angels
This picture belongs to the Detroit Institute of Arts. On its acquisition, in 1957, E. P. Richardson noticed left-handed brush strokes which he took to prove Longhi's privately expressed theory that the work was by Verrocchio, with some collaboration from Leonardo. That theory was accepted by S. Bottari, Morassi, Hendy, and recently Goldscheider. The figure of the Virgin is a mere preparatory sketch.

1960
125 Virgin worshipping the Infant Christ (*The Ruskin Madonna*)
This picture belonged to John Ruskin. It is now in the Sheffield Art Gallery. Berenson [BA 1933] attributed it to Verrocchio, with help from Leonardo and other assistants, and found the technique and artistic quality higher than those of Verrocchio's known works. A. Martini [AF 1960] suggested an attribution to Leonardo alone, at least for the final brushwork ; the preparatory work might have been done by Verrocchio, but modified, and an angel, which J. White could see in the preparation of the composition, had been painted out. This theory aroused great interest on the part of the press, but specialists were far less enthusiastic.

(*From the top*) Madonna with the Cat (*Savona, Noya Collection*). *Autograph drawings for a missing painting; studies* (*pen on grey ground, 128 × 105 mm.; Florence, Uffizi*); *and on white ground, 281 × 199* [*detail*]; *London, British Museum*) (*123*).

Verrocchio workshop: The Virgin and two Angels worshipping the Child (*Detroit, Institute of Arts*) (*124*). (*Below*) The Ruskin Madonna (*Sheffield, Art Gallery*) (*125*).

Appendix I
Leonardo as a sculptor

We learn from the master himself and from other sources that Leonardo tried his hand at sculpture from an early age. While he was Verrocchio's assistant, he certainly had the opportunity of becoming experienced in the techniques of modelling, carving and casting and of following through all its stages the birth of some of the sculptures produced by that very busy workshop. In 1481 he offered his services for the making of an equestrian monument to Francesco Sforza, describing himself as skilled at sculpture in bronze, marble or clay. The commission of that statue, the famous 'horse', was the main reason for his being called to Milan. Again, in 1498, offering his services for the execution of bronze doors for Piacenza Cathedral, he stressed his experience in that field. In Florence, between 1506 and 1511, he helped G. F. Rustici with the making of the clay model of *St John the Baptist between a Pharisee and a Levite* for the Baptistery in Florence (Vasari). Back in Milan, he designed a monument to Giangiacomo Trivulzio, a most impressive scheme (1511–13). Leonardo was mostly interested in bronze sculpture, and he always considered stone carving as inferior to painting, more dependent on technical skill. What attracted him most to working in bronze was the 'scientific' side of casting. It is very difficult to know which part of his preparatory work – for instance his anatomical studies of horses – was 'pure' research for its own sake, and at which point his schemes for the casting of the statue became the study of metallurgy.

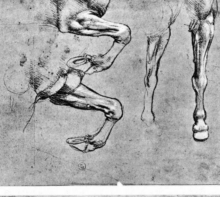

Preparatory studies (ca 1511) for the Trivulzio monument (Windsor, Royal Library [above; and below, right]). This work was intended to stand over the funerary monument of Trivulzio, in the church of S. Celso in Milan. It was never executed. (Below, left) one of the many sketches and the core-frame for the Sforza monument, in the manuscript recently discovered in Madrid.

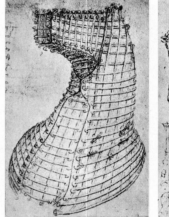

Preparatory sketches (ca 1490) for the Sforza monument (Windsor, Royal Library [above, and below right]; Turin, Biblioteca Reale [above right]). The work on that scheme dragged on from 1483 to 1498, with long interruptions. The first sketch, with the rearing horse, broke with the classic tradition of the equestrian statue. A clay model of the horse alone (double the height of Verrocchio's Colleoni in Venice: about 7 m., according to Luca Pacioli) was exhibited in 1493, but was destroyed shortly afterwards, with the downfall of Lodovico il Moro who had commissioned the work.

Various pieces of sculpture attributed to Leonardo (from the left): Virgin and Child (terracotta, 1470–5; London, Victoria and Albert Museum; from Verrocchio's workshop; attributed to Leonardo by Carotti, Sirén, Valentiner, Middledorf, A. Venturi and others); Id. (stucco relief, ca 1476; London, Jones Collection; Verrocchio workshop, attributed to Leonardo by Mackowsky and A. Venturi); The Pharisee in the group by Rustici (bronze, Florence, Baptistery; this is the part in which Leonardo's intervention seems most likely); Head of an Old Man (Vienna [?], Silbermann Collection; one of the many terracottas attributed to Leonardo's mature period). (Right) Equestrian Group (bronze, height 24 cm.; Budapest, Szépümevészeti Muzeum); among the many similar works (New York, Metropolitan Museum and Frick Collection; Florence, Bargello; Berlin, Staatliche Museen; Milan, Castello Sforzesco; London, British Museum and Jeanneret Collection; Naples, Collezione dell'Arenella; etc.), it is the most widely attributed to Leonardo.

Appendix II
Theoretical and applied research

We can only give here a very small sample of Leonardo's interests, which were universal and included every aspect of knowledge. We have tried above all, on this page, to show his research along lines which were closed to draughtsmanship and which, in accordance with the master's humanistic ideals and with his avowed intentions, used art as a means of scientific research. For instance: his theoretical approach to painting, his research on light, on perspective, anatomy, expression (naturally leading to caricature) and on botany and geology. All those interests are reflected in some of his paintings. The following page shows his scientific and technological speculations: architecture, hydraulics, military engineering, mechanics. They represent a direct link between art and science which we already found in his research on sculpture. Leonardo was also interested in astronomy, mathematics, physics, music, the flight of birds and aeronautics, optics, navigation, voice production and in some of those sciences reached conclusions which have been confirmed by recent discoveries.

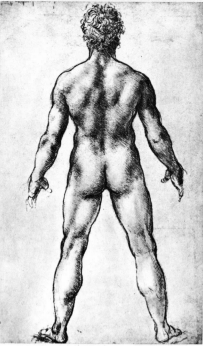

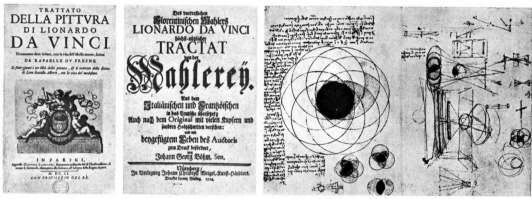

The Trattato della Pittura (*of which we show, above, the frontispiece of the Paris* [1651] *and Nuremberg* [1724] *editions) as we know it now is a posthumous anthology of short notes taken from various autograph manuscripts (such as the studies on the theory of shadows* [C.Atl. 187]*, above, right). The text of the* Trattato *goes back to Francesco Melzi and is contained in a Codex in the Vatican Library. Only an echo of the work as Leonardo had conceived it.*

(*Above*) *drawing of a male nude, from the back* (*Windsor, Royal Library; ca 1503*)*, probably connected with his studies for* The Battle of Anghiari (33). (*Below, from the top*) *a diagram* (*Venice, Accademia; ca 1492*) *derived from* De Architectura *by Vitruvius, showing the proportions of the human body, with notes in the master's handwriting. Anatomical drawing* (*Windsor, Royal Library; ca 1512*) *with autograph notes connected with Leonardo's research with the Paduan scientist M. della Torre.*

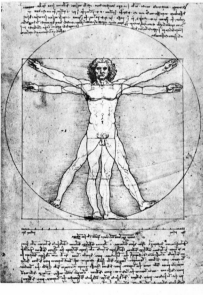

(*Above*) *a sketch of peasants ploughing and sowing* (*Windsor, Royal Library; ca 1500*) *in which Leonardo shows his skill as a master of an open-air 'motif'. (Below) drawing of five grotesque heads* (Ibid.; *ca 1490*) *showing 'types' and much reproduced in the sixteenth and seventeenth centuries, as we know from numerous copies. (Right, from the top) studies of flowers (Venice, Accademia; ca 1485) and of a wild plant and an oak branch (Windsor, Royal Library; ca 1506); the latter can be connected with the lunettes over* The Last Supper (20)*;* [Malaguzzi Valeri] *or* [Bodmer] *with the decoration of the Sala delle Asse (24) in the Castello Sforzesco in Milan.*

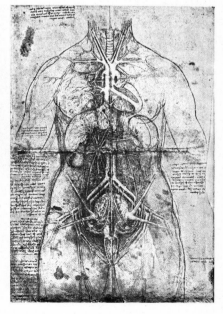

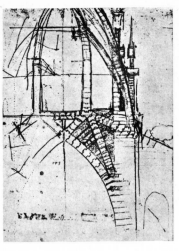

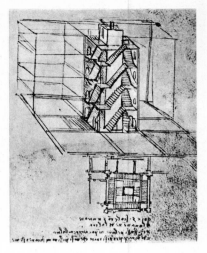

Offering his services (ca 1482) to the Duke of Milan, Leonardo wrote: 'I believe myself able to acquit myself as well as any man in the designing of public and private buildings'. He made designs for (see above left two sketches [C.Atl. 226 and 310 v.]) the cupola of Milan Cathedral, was consulted for Pavia Cathedral and produced ingenious ideas for centrally planned churches (above, middle [Cod. B 17 v.]) and solutions of special problems of interior planning (quadruple staircase, on the right [ld. 47 v.]) for stately homes such as that designed in 1506 for Charles d'Amboise, monumental works (like the scheme for a bridge over the Bosphorus studied in 1502 for the Sultan Bajazet II), and surprisingly functional urban structures (streets on an upper level, here on the right [ld. 36 and 16 v.]) which are often the precursors of modern ideas by Le Corbusier and other innovators. (Below, left) project for the casting of a gigantic cannon (Windsor, Royal Library).

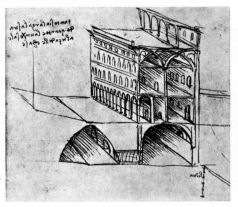
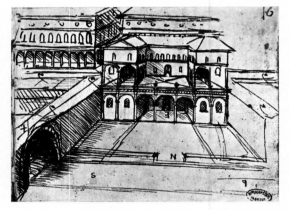

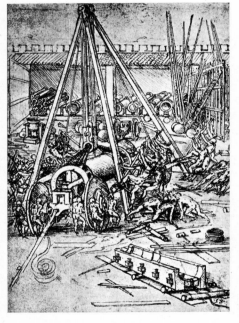
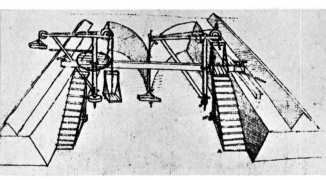
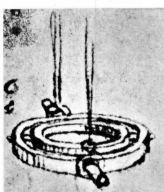

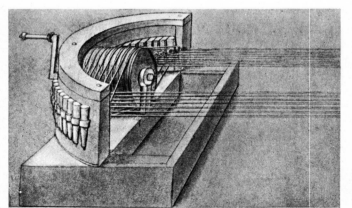

(Left, from the top) study for a machine to lift and carry material in the excavating of a canal (C. Atl. 363 v.). Sketch for a capstan with fifteen spindles (ld. 2 v.). Explosive grenades and shield-bows (Paris, École des Beaux Arts). (Above) drawing of a ring with cardan suspension (C. Atl. 288). (Below) study of a device for underwater swimming (ld., 7).

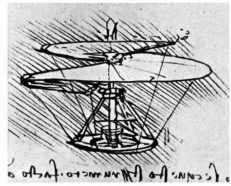

Project for rotary flying machine reminiscent of a helicopter (Cod. B 83 v.).

Subject Index

This index deals with recurrent 'motifs' in Leonardo's work, which do not constitute the principal themes (which may be found in the Title Index) and relates to the paintings contained in the catalogue from 1 to 37 ·

Title Index

The asterisk on the right of the number indicates the existence of variants or copies of the same subject, taken into account in the caption to which the number refers

Location Index

For possible or supposed derivations of lost pictures or of pictures formerly attributed to the Master or whose attribution is no longer credited, see preceding Index.